"Are y

he dem~~anded~~, ~~catching her~~ by the shoulders and looking into her eyes. "I heard you scream."

"I...I'm..." she began, but the sight of him like that made it hard for her to speak. He looked as though he was ready to fight whoever or whatever dared to cause her harm, ready to take on the unseen enemy on her behalf. She'd never in her life had someone step forward to defend her in such a way. She was stunned, grateful, excited...too many emotions to sort through in the short span of time. Now, as they stood opposite each other in that tiny bathroom, with Cade's strong hands gripping her arms, all she could do was stare at him. He was breathing hard, his eyes swirling with emotion as they bore into hers, and she suddenly found herself unable to resist.

Before she could stop herself, she leaned forward... and kissed him.

"Are you okay? What happened?"

PROTECTIVE ASSIGNMENT

JANIE CROUCH

Harlequin

INTRIGUE

This book is dedicated to the gals like me
who have been reading Harlequin's great books since we were teens
stuffing as many into our bag as we could check out from the library.

Harlequin®
INTRIGUE™

Recycling programs
for this product may
not exist in your area.

ISBN-13: 978-1-335-69015-9

Protective Assignment

 Harlequin Enterprises ULC
22 Adelaide St. West, 41st Floor
Toronto, Ontario M5H 4E3, Canada
www.Harlequin.com

Printed in Lithuania

MIX
Paper | Supporting
responsible forestry
FSC® C021394

Janie Crouch writes passionate romantic suspense for readers who still believe in heroes. After a lifetime on the East Coast—and a six-year stint in Germany—this *USA TODAY* bestselling author has settled into her dream home in the Front Range of the Colorado Rockies. She loves engaging in all sorts of adventures (triathlons! two-hundred-mile relay races! mountain treks!), traveling and surviving life with four kids. You can find out more about her at janiecrouch.com.

Books by Janie Crouch

Harlequin Intrigue

Warrior Peak Sanctuary

Protective Assignment

San Antonio Security

Texas Bodyguard: Luke
Texas Bodyguard: Brax
Texas Bodyguard: Weston
Texas Bodyguard: Chance

The Risk Series: A Bree and Tanner Thriller

Calculated Risk
Security Risk
Constant Risk
Risk Everything

Omega Sector: Under Siege

Daddy Defender
Protector's Instinct
Cease Fire

Visit the Author Profile page
at Harlequin.com for more titles.

CAST OF CHARACTERS

Cade Thatcher—Former soldier nearly killed in a mission-gone-wrong two years ago. He's coming to finish the last of his rehab at Warrior Peak Sanctuary and start fresh as the tactical missions team leader.

River Robertson—On the run from the cult she was raised in and the leader who wants her for his wife.

Xavier Michaels—Former CIA agent and co-owner of Warrior Peak Sanctuary who runs the day-to-day operations of the center.

Lawson Davies—Former Army Special Forces and co-owner of Warrior Peak Sanctuary who runs their tactical unit.

Hannah Davies—Lawson's younger sister who works at Warrior Peak Sanctuary and is always ready to help with a friendly smile.

Chapter One

Cade Thatcher drummed his fingers on the steering wheel and sighed as he made the turn off the main highway and onto the long, winding mountain road that would lead him to the Warrior Peak Sanctuary.

Was this really a good idea? It wasn't as though he had much of a choice. Right now, it was the only option he had if he didn't want to sit around home feeling like he was losing his mind for the next few months as he finished his recovery.

And seeing his brother would be a good thing, right?

When Carter suggested he come up and visit for a while, he had been reluctant, but he hadn't had any better options come along lately, so he'd decided to accept the offer. It would be a change, being with his actual brother instead of the brothers-in-arms he had worked with in the military, but he needed to get used to his new life, his new body and his new existence after his injuries.

A shock of pain raced down his arm and he winced, releasing his suddenly tight grip on the steering wheel. He needed to remember to stay loose and relaxed. Any sudden tension in his neck and shoulders still caused some discomfort, sometimes even stealing his breath. It had been getting better the last few weeks, but there were still moments where it really stung. His doctors were just impressed that he had managed to recover as well as he had, but he was still frustrated at the pain that seemed to get the better of him now and then.

When he'd first woken up in that hospital bed, the doctors hadn't been enthusiastic about his chances of ever making a full recovery. He could still remember, all too vividly, the look on that one doctor's face when she had told him how bad things were. His shoulder, broken in several places from taking a bullet, damage to his lower back and basically his entire body from shrapnel, then head damage to top it all off. He hadn't been able to move, let alone think straight. His whole body swollen and in constant pain, as he tried to wrap his head around what had happened. And even that was hard with the huge gaps of missing time and memories he had tried to recall. He'd always known working in the military was risky, but this? This was the kind of thing he hadn't been ready for at all. It was downright terrifying.

They hadn't been sure if he was going to be able to use that arm again or even walk when it was all said and done, but he had defied the odds. Not a chance in hell he was going to sit around the rest of his life. Even if he couldn't fight or be with his brothers-in-arms again, he could still do something. Still be useful in some capacity, help make a difference in some way. He'd thrown himself into physical therapy, trying to get control of his shattered bones and aching muscles once more. He wasn't going to let his life fall away from him just because of one injury.

And now he was back on his feet. Only literally, of

course, because he felt like the rest of his world had collapsed around him. He had wanted to be a soldier for as long as he could remember. From the day he graduated high school, he had focused all his time and energy on what he could achieve and on building the strong bonds he had with the other guys in his unit. But now?

Now he was floundering with no clear direction, not knowing what came next. Unable to do the one thing he'd always wanted and been good at had left a huge void he didn't know how to fill. Now that he was close to fully recovered, he had to figure out what his life looked like on the other side of healing.

The drive up to the lodge was quiet and scenic and empty; no other cars passed and not even a building lined the side of the road. Just forest for as far as the eye could see. In fact, there wouldn't have been anything to break up the monotony at all, if it hadn't been for her.

Cade furrowed his brow when he spotted her on the side of the road. What was she doing out here in the middle of nowhere? A woman, wearing a long dress that covered almost every inch of her body, with her thumb held out like she was hitchhiking. She couldn't have had much luck out there, given how few cars there were on the road. She had an old-school military backpack, stuffed to the brim, slung over one shoulder, and as Cade drew closer, he could see it had seen some serious action.

He slowed his truck down and pulled over to the side as he reached her.

"Hey," he called to her, rolling the passenger window down. "You okay? You lost?"

"I'm not lost," she replied, a little curtly. "I need a lift."

"Your car broken down or something?" he replied, glancing around to see if there was another vehicle he hadn't spotted. She shook her head.

"I'm heading north," she explained. "You going that way?"

"I am, but just as far as the Warrior Peak Sanctuary," he replied. "That enough for you?"

She hesitated for a moment, eyes darting around, but then nodded. "That works."

"Come on in," he told her, reaching over to open the passenger-side door. She readjusted the backpack over her shoulder and hurried to the door, slipping into the seat next to him. Outside, the sky had started to darken and rain began to pour, one of those North Carolina cloudbursts that seemed to come out of nowhere.

"Looks like I timed that well," he remarked, and she gave him a tight smile, holding her pack tight on her lap, like she was trying to use it as a shield to protect herself. Cade quickly glanced in the rearview mirror, then over his shoulder before he pulled the truck back on to the road, and continued up the mountain toward the lodge.

"You hitchhiked the whole way up here?" he asked, trying to fill the strained silence between them.

She nodded again.

"If you need to charge your phone—" he began, but she cut him off before he could go any further.

"I don't have a phone," she replied, shaking her head.

He noticed that she was shivering slightly. The dress she wore obviously hadn't provided much coverage from the elements, and he thought about offering her his jacket, but he doubted she would take it. He reached over to adjust the heat settings instead and noticed her tense and shift closer to the door, like she was ready to bolt at a moment's notice. She also looked disheveled and tired, as if she'd been out in the wilderness for a while. Was she in some kind of trouble? A young woman on the side of the road like that, hitchhiking—it didn't seem like a good situation.

"I can call someone for you, if you want," he offered, and she jumped slightly at the sudden sound of his voice before shaking her head again, her eyes fixed on the window.

"It's fine," she replied, and he turned his attention back to the road, his mind racing as he tried to make sense of the situation.

"I'm Cade, by the way. Cade Thatcher," he told her, hoping to put her at ease, and maybe get some information out of her in the process.

She paused for a moment like she wasn't certain she wanted to tell him her name. "River," she replied finally, nodding in greeting.

River. Interesting name.

"Where you from, River?" he asked, trying to keep the conversation going.

"Florida."

"You're a long way from home," he remarked. "What brings you north?"

"Just needed a change," she replied, looking down to the bag on her lap again. He frowned. Was it him or was she seriously wary of making small talk? Almost like she was afraid she'd let something slip if she had a conversation with him.

Cade couldn't stop his mind from running through possible scenarios. What was she doing in the woods by herself? Was she getting out of a bad situation? On the run from someone? Judging by her simple, understated look—longer hair, her plain homemade dress, no makeup, no piercings or jewelry—maybe she had been in some kind of cult.

Or maybe he had been watching too much TV these last several months. He hadn't had a whole lot else to do since his discharge from the military aside from concentrating on his therapy. He kept his eyes on the road, and figured he should let her catch her breath before he started interrogating her. It really wasn't his business, but he couldn't help being curious. It wasn't far to the lodge, and maybe he could get a little more out of her then. If she was willing to share.

Finally, the road led them past the Warrior Peak Sanctuary sign to a big, sprawling complex that hung on to the top of the mountain for dear life, surrounded by trees and with a view down over the forest below. Cade climbed out of the truck, grabbed an umbrella from under the seat and went around to open her door. But before he could, it swung open and nearly hit him in the face as she hurried to get out. He shot out his hand to grab it before it could make contact.

"You should go inside and warm up," he suggested as she hooked the backpack over her shoulders again and tried to contain a shiver. He opened up the umbrella and held it out to her.

She hesitantly reached out to take it from him and eyed him skeptically, as if trying to decide if she should trust him.

"There'll be plenty of people in the lodge who'll be heading north soon enough that you could ask for a ride. You can't stand out here in this rain—you'll get soaked to the bone, probably end up sick too," he pointed out as he stepped around her to get his bag out of the back.

He hadn't packed a whole lot, just a large duffel and his backpack; his brother had told him he wouldn't need it. Anything he was missing he could get there at the lodge or he could make a run into the small town below.

He held up his old military backpack and grinned at her. "Look, we match."

For the first time since he'd laid eyes on her, a smile spread over her face. Cade was momentarily stunned.

With a smile on her face, she looked like a whole different person. Those huge blue eyes lit up, and dimples appeared on her cheeks; even though she looked as though she had been living in the woods for the past few years, she was seriously beautiful.

Cade stared at her for a long moment before he pulled himself together again. He was curious to find out more about her, and he hoped he could convince her to stick around for at least a night before she took off to wherever she was headed. Shaking his head to clear it, he reached for the umbrella and held it over the two of them as they walked toward the entrance.

She hung back behind him as he made his way to the huge wooden doors of the lodge, and he chanced a glance over his shoulder at her. There was a flash of fear in her eyes, and his heart twisted seeing her like that. He might not have known what she was running from, but at least he could try to get her to stay the night out of the weather where she could rest and take some time to settle down, right?

"Come on in," he told her. "There's a cafeteria in there,

and there's probably a spare room you can use to sleep for the night."

She frowned. She still didn't look convinced, but out here, in the middle of nowhere, what choice did she have?

"It's freezing out here," he reminded her. "And you saw those roads—nobody else is going to be coming up here tonight. You should get some food in you and rest, okay?"

He could practically see her mind racing as she tried to figure out what the best course of action was. But when she looked up to the sky, it seemed to settle her decision. The rain was set to continue for the rest of the night, judging by the thick gray clouds drifting off into the horizon, and it was starting to get dark. She could stand out on the side of the road for the rest of the night in the hopes some passerby would take her another few miles toward her destination.

Or, she could follow him inside the lodge for a warm meal and a warm bed.

Her shoulders slumped as she let out a resigned sigh and followed him into the welcoming warmth of the lodge.

Chapter Two

River Robertson felt herself shrinking as she stepped through the large doors of the lodge, glancing around and taking in her surroundings. This place was nice—really nice. Way nicer than anything she was used to, and she was sure she stuck out like a sore thumb. She looked like a drowned rat that had been running wild in the woods for a while. She didn't belong here.

She hung back next to the door, still clutching her backpack to her like a protective shield, as a pretty woman behind the front desk rushed out to greet Cade. Her heels tapped on the polished wooden floor, echoing around the open space. The whole place looked like it was made of the same material, practically glistening in the dim golden light from the fixtures around the walls. It looked warm and welcoming.

"Cade, there you are!" the woman exclaimed. She pulled him into a hug and then called over her shoulder. "Carter, Cade's here!"

A few moments later, another man stepped out from a room behind the front desk, and paused for a moment as he looked Cade up and down. He was similar in build and looks, so…brothers, maybe.

"Where have you been, man?" he demanded. "You're late."

"I know, I know," Cade replied, waving a hand.

"It's the weather," the woman cut in. "It's probably made the roads really difficult, right, Cade?"

"Something like that," he agreed.

"You know how to handle the weather," Carter remarked, shaking his head. "How's your shoulder? You doing okay?"

"I'm fine," Cade shot back, as though it was the last thing he wanted to talk about. Nobody seemed to notice River standing next to the door, but she was fine with that. This way, she got a chance to scope out the people around her and get a feel for their dynamic, whether or not she would really be safe here.

Cade was right, she wasn't exactly going to have much luck waiting for another ride tonight in the pouring rain, but that didn't mean she had any intention of letting her guard down.

Not here, not anywhere.

The three of them talked a little more about the weather and about the drive up.

River looked around, doing her best to take in every detail she could. She had hoped she could make it a little farther north tonight, but she doubted anyone else would have pulled over for her, especially with her looking like she did. Heck, it was a miracle Cade had stopped. She wasn't sure why he had decided to take pity on her, but she was relieved for a chance to get out of the cold for a while.

Finally, the woman glanced over and did a double take when she saw River almost plastered to the wall by the door. She frowned, concern evident in her expression. River was used to that look by now, even if she never intentionally gave someone a reason to stare at her.

"Oh. I'm sorry. Who are you?" the woman asked, turning toward her, and Cade quickly jumped in.

"This is River," he explained. "I gave her a lift up here. She was out on the road hitchhiking."

"Hitchhiking? In this weather?" Carter asked, concern and confusion crossing his face.

River didn't blame him. The roads had been almost deserted, and she couldn't imagine anyone in their right mind would be hitchhiking in the freezing-cold rain.

"This is my brother Carter and our friend Hannah Davies," Cade continued introductions. "Hannah runs the front desk and Carter's a physical therapist here at the lodge."

Carter glanced over at Cade, and River felt her shoulders tense slightly and her legs lock in anticipation to move. She wasn't sure exactly what they were communicating to each other with that look, but she didn't like it—didn't like not knowing. Her eyes darted between them, and she moved toward the door, ready to make a run for it at any moment.

But before she could, Hannah stepped forward, smiling at her. "Come on, let's see if we can find you a shower and some dry clothes while these two catch up."

River shot a panicked look to Cade, who nodded and gave her a friendly smile. "I'll catch up with you in a bit, okay?"

She nodded in Cade's direction as Hannah took River's arm and steered her toward a door at the far side of the lobby. As she let the woman lead her through the halls of the lodge, her eyes darted around, checking out the exits, her avenues of escape. If she needed to make a break for it, then she was going to be prepared, just like she always was.

After a couple more turns, Hannah stopped outside one of the dozen or so doorways in the long corridor they'd been walking down. River peered around Hannah to the far end, checking to see how far it was to the nearest exit. She didn't see an actual door, but there was a large window at the end of the hall that would work as an escape route in an emergency, if necessary.

"It's so nice to have another female around," Hannah said cheerfully, like she didn't notice River's distraction. "Sometimes it feels like the walls of this place just drip with testosterone, you know? Anyway, this room is free, so let's get you settled."

River turned her attention back to Hannah, and followed her into the room where they'd stopped. Hannah held out the key card she'd used to unlock the door, dropping it into River's hand. "This gets you in and out of your room, so make sure to keep it with you. Everything else is either open or has a flip lock on the door."

Hannah glanced around the room. "So, here you go. I think this should do you for tonight, at least. I know it's not much, but there's a fresh-made bed and you won't have to be out there in the rain, right?"

"Right," River quietly agreed, tucking the key card into the pocket of her long skirt and looking around more.

Even if Hannah didn't seem that impressed with the room, River liked it. Like the rest of the lodge, the room had dark wood floors and walls giving it a wooded, cozy feel. The few pictures decorating the walls looked as though they were of the surrounding forest, all green trees as far as the eye could see, some including wildlife. She approached the window and peered outside. It gave her a view down over the main road she and Cade drove up on, which was a relief. She would be able to keep an eye on anyone coming and going from this place, which would give her an advantage if…

If anything happened.

She tried to push that to the back of her mind as Hannah explained how the different remotes for the TV mounted on the wall worked and how to get the bedside light on. It was the closest thing River had come to a real home for a while, but she still felt like she was holding her breath as she tried to take it all in.

"You okay?" Hannah asked, and River nodded quickly.

"I know it's a lot," she remarked, laughing. "Sorry about dropping all of this on you. Oh, one more thing. If you want a shower, they're at the end of the hall in this section of the lodge. It's a huge, shared, locker-room-style bathroom. There're two different sides—men and women, and the doors lock on each in designated areas. The guys normally don't care about seeing each other naked, but just make sure you push the latch all the way across on the women's side, okay?"

"I will," River agreed.

"Okay, you get yourself settled, and I'll bring up some fresh towels and toiletries for you," she told her. "You need some fresh clothes, too?"

"Yeah, I think so," River replied, glancing down at her wet dress. She wasn't even sure how long she'd been wearing it, but it seemed nothing short of a miracle it had lasted as long as it had. The few other things she had with her she'd grabbed from a donation bin in Tennessee. She didn't even know if they'd fit her, but they really needed to be laundered before she wore them. She just hadn't found a place to do that yet.

"No problem, let me see what I can do," Hannah said with a small wave as she walked out the door, closing it behind her and leaving River in silence once more.

River walked around the room she was going to be staying in, taking in every detail she could. She had no idea who these people really were, no idea what kind of place this was, and she wasn't going to let her guard down just because they seemed friendly enough. She checked all the lights for hidden cameras, pulling open the closet and peering around to make sure there was no way they could be watching her. There was a mirror on the closet door, so no way they could have two-way glass, but she would check in the bathroom when she went down there.

Once she was certain she wasn't being watched, she started to unpack her bag. Not that there was much to unpack. A water filtration kit, a couple of tattered maps, a compass she wasn't even certain actually pointed north anymore, and the handful of donated clothes along with the extra set of shoes she had managed to swipe too, even though they barely fit her.

Buried at the bottom was her sleeping bag, which was basically torn to shreds. She would never have been able to sleep in it outside tonight, not with the rain that poured down beyond the window. She had been using it for weeks now, and she was surprised the cheap thing had held up that long, but it wasn't as though she'd had much of a choice about where she could rest. She'd been out on the road this whole time, sleeping in the elements, and anything that could give her a little cover was a welcome change.

Pulling open the drawers, she continued her search for anything that might indicate she was in trouble and needed to leave. She stuck her hand into them, feeling around for a false bottom, but nothing was there.

She slumped back on to the bed, catching her breath, and a sudden wave of exhaustion hit her so hard she could feel her eyes drooping on the spot. She brushed it off quickly. She couldn't let her guard down, no matter what kind of place this seemed to be. She knew better than that: she had to stay alert and aware if she was going to make it to Haven. She had to keep her head on straight, and not let the comfortable coziness of this room get to her.

A knock sounded at the door, and she jumped to her feet once more.

"Hey!" Hannah called brightly through the door. "Here's your stuff. Help yourself to a shower whenever you want, okay?"

"Okay!" River called back, hoping she would leave her alone sooner rather than later. She was nervous enough being in this new place, and adding new faces and conversations in the mix was just draining. She was used to only having herself for company, not having to talk to others. They seemed friendly enough, though, especially Hannah. But she was ready to have a few minutes alone to adjust and settle in.

She was still hesitant to stay. She was so used to being on the run, River wasn't sure if she'd be able to let that feeling go. But she could take advantage of their kindness for a night, couldn't she? Just one night. She could be out on the road again first thing the next morning, but she needed to wash, to warm up, and to get a decent night's sleep. Maybe even some food if she could find some.

Reaching back into her bag, she felt around for the knife—her father's knife. Feeling the cool blade under her fingers, she pulled it out and stared at the sharp, serrated edge. This would have to keep her safe, at least for now. She hoped she wouldn't have to use it, but there was no way to tell, not yet.

She ran her finger along the blade lightly, comforting herself with the reminder of what she could do with it if she needed to. Pushing the knife into the pocket of her dress, she listened until she was sure that Hannah's footsteps had retreated down the hallway once more before opening the door. She glanced down the corridor both ways, ensuring nobody was watching her, and then grabbed for the towels, toiletries and the clothes Hannah had left outside her door. Shaking them out, she checked to see if there were any devices hidden in the folds, but she couldn't see anything. Then she turned to dig around in the toiletry bag as well, also finding nothing.

With the weight of the knife in her pocket, she hurried down the hallway toward the showers.

One night. This is just for one night.

These people probably didn't mean her any harm. And if they did, they had no idea who they were dealing with— no idea what she was capable of.

Or how far she would go to survive.

Chapter Three

Carter placed his plate on the table opposite to his brother—roast beef, mashed potatoes and a healthy serving of greens on the side—and sank down into his seat.

"Well, now that you're finally here, are you going to tell me how you're really doing?" he said gruffly.

Cade grinned. He knew it was the closest he was ever going to get to a friendly greeting from his brother. That had just always been Carter's way with him, ever since he joined the military, and doubly so since he'd been injured. He knew it was Carter's way of showing he cared, though, and he appreciated it.

"Not too bad," he replied. "Glad to get up here for a while. Felt like the walls were closing in and I was feeling a bit useless, stewing down there at home."

"You're not useless," Carter replied at once. "You're injured. You need plenty of time to get back on your feet after what happened, you know that."

"I know." Cade sighed, picking at the food in front of him—the same dinner as Carter had on his plate, but he didn't feel too hungry right now.

He used to have a heck of an appetite, eating everything that was put in front of him, but that was when he had been in training and in combat. His body had needed all the support and sustenance it could get to keep him going.

But that had been before.

Before the injury, before he'd had to give up the one thing that had driven him forward and given him purpose. He'd taken a heavy beating in combat between his shoulder, scattered shrapnel in his body and his skull nearly being split in half that he'd had to relearn basically everything since then.

How to walk, how to talk, how to move, how to say his own name.

There were still memories from before the injury and of his time in the hospital that were hazy, but he knew he'd come a hell of a long way since the moment he'd woken up with his whole life tipped upside down.

At least when he was in recovery, he'd had something to focus on. He needed something moving him forward, and learning how to get his life back had given him that meaning for a while.

But now?

Now he craved the thrill of active duty, and the camaraderie of his life with the guys in his unit. Being stuck with an injury and far from the action was making him feel a little crazy.

"You're doing good, Cade," Carter told him. "Think about where you were just last year—"

"I try not to," Cade replied, cutting him off before he could go any further. "Anyway, you mind me taking advantage of the family discount?"

"How do you mean?" Carter asked, furrowing his brow.

"For the physical therapy," he replied. "I mean, I need

to get back in shape, right? The VA hardly covers what I need to get back out in the—"

"Why do you even want to get back out there again? How do you even know if you can?" Carter asked, and Cade could sense his irritation. "You had a head injury, for crying out loud. That's something to take seriously. You're lucky to have survived." He furrowed his brow and snapped his mouth shut to keep from saying more.

Cade couldn't blame his brother for his response to his wishful plan. Carter had seen a lot while helping him get back on his feet. He couldn't hold it against him that he didn't want Cade to walk right back into the setting that had landed him in all this trouble in the first place. His recovery hadn't been a pretty situation to be around, and Cade certainly wasn't the best company during the worst of his injuries.

"Hey, it's not for you to know why," he joked back. "You just have to do your job, right?"

Truth be told, he was dodging the question. First off, he didn't even know if he'd be allowed back after the injuries he suffered. Probably not, but he could still hold on to that dream a little longer. Secondly, he didn't want to admit to his brother the truth—that he felt useless, hopeless, in the state he was in now. He couldn't just sit around doing nothing for the rest of his life. He needed that hit of adrenaline, the thrill that came with the life he used to have, and he was never going to get it watching true crime documentaries on repeat in his apartment.

He wasn't the man he used to be, and he hated it. He wasn't sure how much longer he could keep living the way he was, and he hoped his brother, who had been working as a physical therapist for the last few years, would be able to get him back on his feet and ready to get out there again. Deep down Cade knew he wouldn't be able to do what he did before with his unit, but there had to be something in some related capacity that could get him back out there, let him feel that rush again. Feel like he was contributing to something that mattered.

But before the conversation could go any further, they were joined by another diner, Xavier Michaels, former CIA, and also one of the owners of the lodge. He cracked a beer as he slid into an empty chair, grinning at Cade in greeting.

"Hey, there," he said. "Didn't expect you to make it here."

"What, to the lodge?" Cade asked.

"No, to your thirties," he replied.

"Trust me, I made a damn good try not to," Cade chuckled, earning a scowl from his brother. But before he could say anything else, the floor creaked behind them. He glanced over and saw River, peering around the cafeteria, looking as pale as a ghost.

She wore a sweater and a pair of ill-fitting jeans. Her hair was pulled up in a ponytail at the top of her head and hung down her back, and she clutched a tray of food like it was the only thing keeping her pinned to the earth.

"That the hitchhiker?" Xavier asked, lifting his chin in her direction, as she went to find a seat on the far side of the room from the guys.

Carter nodded. "Yeah, the one Cade picked up," he replied. "Any idea who she is, by the way, Cade?"

"None," Cade answered, watching as she sat at one of the tables with her back against the wall so she could keep an eye on the room. "Thanks for giving her a place to stay tonight, Xavier. I appreciate it."

"Hey, it was Hannah's doing, but I'm not one to turn away a woman in the middle of nowhere who looks like she's been on the road for months already." Xavier shrugged.

"Where do you think she's from?" Carter asked.

"Not from around here, that's for sure," Xavier replied. "But anyone on the side of the road out there at this time of the year isn't doing it for fun. She's trying to get away from something, I'd bet. Or someone."

"We need to quit staring, guys. She's skittish enough without seeing us watching her," Cade commented as he got to his feet, grabbing his tray and heading over to join River. It would give him a chance to deflect his brother's questions about what he was planning to do now that he was out here. He also wanted to find out what was going on with her if he could. Maybe even help.

Those giant blue eyes darted up to look at him as he drew closer, and she clenched the cutlery in her hand a little tighter.

"Mind if I join you?" he asked, gesturing to the spot opposite her.

She shook her head. "Go ahead," she replied, and he planted himself down in the chair across from her.

She picked at her food for a few moments, staring down at the plate in front of her as though it held the mysteries to the universe.

Cade snuck glances at her while he had a few bites of his own meal. Taking in her slim build and tired eyes. He could tell she was struggling to get by and running on exhaustion.

Xavier was right, there was no way she was out here by choice. She had to be running from something. Judging by her jumpy demeanor, she clearly hadn't put as much distance as she'd have liked between herself and whatever was after her.

"Are you in some kind of trouble?" he asked her finally.

She startled, lifting her gaze to meet his. "You ask all the girls that?" she shot back, but a whisper of a smile passed over her lips as she spoke.

He grinned back at her, hoping they could break the ice. It was clear this woman had some serious nerve, and he was eager to find out if there was more of it to come once she got some food in her and proper rest.

"Where you headed?" he asked, deciding to try a different approach.

She shrugged. "Wherever I need to end up," she replied, pushing food around on her plate.

She wasn't going to make this easy for him, that much he could tell for sure. If he couldn't get her to talk about herself, maybe he could, at least, make her feel a little more at ease.

"You're safe here," he said gently. "You know much about the lodge?"

She shook her head, finally taking a real bite of her food.

"It's a place that helps people with military or law enforcement experience get back on their feet after they've had an injury, physical or mental," he told her. "Everyone here, they're on the right side of the law. You're not in danger here, River. It's one of the safest places you could be."

She took another bite of her food, and then stirred the potatoes around on her plate before she responded.

"I don't really know where I'm going after this," she admitted to him finally. Her voice sounded small, almost shaky, and Cade frowned. He saw dark circles under her eyes, and her cheeks looked a little sunken, as though it had been a long time since she'd had a decent meal. How long had she been living like this?

He held himself back from asking that question, not wanting to overwhelm her or give her a reason to stop talking. She was eating now and going to be able to get a good night's sleep—that was what mattered.

Soon enough, she had finished her food. He could tell she was still hungry, though, and he pushed his plate over to her. She glanced up at him, her eyes flashing with embarrassment. It was clear she wasn't used to asking for what she wanted or needed from people, but he intended to change that, if he could.

"You can stay here as long as you need to. These guys won't mind," he told her, tilting his head to the guys at the other table. "And you need to eat and get some rest. Otherwise, whatever you're running from is going to catch up with you, and you're not going to have the strength to defend yourself from it, right?"

She chewed on her lip for a moment, but then reached for his plate. Something seemed to have clicked with her. Cade nodded and got to his feet to leave her to finish up and grab some more food for himself. Once he had a full plate, he returned to the other table where Carter and Xavier had been watching their exchange the whole time.

"Well? Find anything out?" his brother asked.

Cade nodded. "She looks to be in her midtwenties, and

she's from Florida. That's what she told me on the ride up here. Didn't give me a city or anything, but it's something."

"Her name's River, right?" Carter asked.

"Or that's her alias," Cade replied. "She didn't volunteer a last name. You think we could get someone to look into missing person reports from Florida for the last few months?"

"You think she's actually in trouble?" Xavier asked, raising his eyebrows. "Not just trying to get away from a boyfriend or her family?"

"I don't know," Cade replied, shaking his head. "She's been out on the road for a while by looking at her, with just the ratty bag she has with her. She looks malnourished and tired. Like she's been surviving out there by herself. I doubt she realized how quiet the road up to this place is, and she seems…anxious. Flighty."

Cade fell silent as he watched Hannah approach River. The woman looked uneasy, ready to bolt, her face taut even as sweet, bubbly Hannah tried to talk to her. It was obvious she wasn't going to let anyone get close to her, at least not yet. That only spurred Cade's interest even more.

"Well, she can stay," Xavier said, looking in River's direction. "And I'll do what I can with the little information we have to see if there's anything we can find out about her. But if there's any trouble from her—or if she brings any trouble to the lodge—she's out, okay? I can't have anyone bringing that kind of chaos here. It would jeopardize everything we do here."

"Thanks, Xavier," Cade replied.

He watched as Hannah and River talked. There was something about her that had captured his attention, some instinct deep inside he couldn't ignore that told him she was in trouble. And he wanted to help.

He was going to get to the bottom of it.

Chapter Four

River hurried back down to her room as soon as she had finished her second plate of food, hoping they didn't think she was being greedy. At first, she was hesitant to accept Cade's plate that he pushed toward her, but she was so hungry and the food tasted so good. It was the first decent meal she'd had in weeks. She wouldn't have any more meals like that once she got back out on the road, so she'd taken his advice and dug in before he changed his mind.

She couldn't help but notice the others in the eating area sneaking glances at her while she ate and especially when Cade joined her. She knew they were curious and wanted to ask questions, and she appreciated that they mostly kept their distance—apart from Cade and Hannah. She didn't want to draw more attention to herself than she already had. She needed to do better. If someone came looking for her specifically or asking questions about a stranger and gave her description, she'd be in trouble.

She kept bouncing the idea around in her head to stay. If she decided to, and she really did want to, she couldn't afford for people to ask her questions, especially since she could not give them any true answers. She'd need to lie, and she didn't want to do that. Out on the road, she had been running for her life, doing everything she could just to make it from one day to the next. Would a few days here really be that bad?

Even though Hannah had offered to get her a coffee so the two of them could talk, River had excused herself and returned to her room, locking the door behind her and sliding the wooden chair from the desk against it to make it a little harder to open. Force of habit—she would always think about protecting herself, no matter what the circumstances she found herself in happened to be.

She perched on the edge of the bed, looking out the window to the parking lot to make sure she didn't miss anyone trying to make their approach. She wasn't going to let anyone get the jump on her, even if Cade had gone out of his way to try and assure her this place was safe. She didn't trust him yet, though—she didn't trust anyone, not when it came to getting where she needed to go.

But this place…it seemed like it made sense for her to arrive here. It was like a rehab, right? A place where people could come to fix themselves up after they'd been through hell. Ironic that she could probably use some of the help they offered, but she wasn't going to stick around long enough to take advantage of it. They would probably get tired of giving her sanctuary soon enough anyway, especially when they realized she wouldn't be able to pay them.

That was not a problem, though. She'd get back out on the road, keep moving, and she could work on whatever she needed to when she had finally arrived at her end goal. She wasn't going to let the fact that she didn't exactly know *where* that was stop her journey.

She pulled the knife from where she had stashed it in

the pocket of the jeans Hannah had brought up for her. It felt good to be in clean clothes after so long, even if they didn't really fit. Just being able to shower and eat had been a weight off her shoulders. The roast beef she'd had tonight had been the best thing she'd ever tasted. Even though her stomach was full, her mouth still watered for more.

Her eyes started to get heavy, and she wrapped her fingers tighter around the knife as she began to doze off. She knew she needed to rest, but it was hard to let go of the control she had been hanging on to for so long, even for a single night. She knew that she was relatively safe at the moment, but letting down her guard after months of her body being in fight-or-flight mode was hard to do.

Eventually, though, she nodded off with the knife still grasped in her hand, until she was woken with a start by the sound of engines in the parking lot.

She sprang up, eyes wide and heart racing, and darted to the window to peer into the parking lot. The first light of dawn was already filtering through the trees. A couple of cars had arrived, along with a large van. A handful of what looked to be hikers climbed out, spilling into the parking lot. Her eyes scanned the faces, trying to see if she recognized any of them. She searched for a familiar gait, someone looking up at the window for her, anything, but none of them seemed familiar, or to be paying any attention to her.

She relaxed her stance but continued to look around the lot. It was getting busy; there would be too many people around soon. She needed to leave. She had no way to control who came in and out of this place, and that scared her more than she wanted to admit. How could she ever really feel safe if she was constantly second-guessing every person who stepped through the door?

Sliding her gaze past the crowd approaching the entrance, she spotted a row of bikes at the far end of the parking lot. That would do. She could steal one of them, take off, and she would be gone before anyone even noticed. But one look at the gray skies above told her that wouldn't be a good idea. She wouldn't get far before the weather turned again, and then, where would she be? Soaked through, back out in the middle of nowhere with no idea how long it would be before another driver was kind enough to pick her up and take her a little farther down the road. And she had no idea if the next one would be as kind as Cade seemed to be.

She sighed and sat back down on the bed, running her fingers over the blade of the knife again. She could stay for a few days, right? Just a little longer. Until the weather cleared, at least. She could get some supplies, make sure she had a decent amount of food in her stomach, and then move on. Give herself a better fighting chance to be full and rested.

As though agreeing, her stomach grumbled pointedly. She needed to get something to eat. Would the cafeteria be open this early? She didn't think to check for times. She wanted to take advantage of being here as much as she could, no matter how much her instincts were telling her to stay hidden in her room. Eventually, she knew Hannah or Cade would come looking for her, though, so better not to. She would just do better at keeping a low profile, stay out of the way.

In reality, she knew she had already failed at that. What with Cade bringing her here and Hannah trying to befriend her. If it hadn't been for him, she would have been out there all night, in the pouring rain, freezing and probably ending up sick. Who knew if she would even have survived another night out in the cold like that? Her body was getting frailer with every passing day. With no proper food or sleep and always ready to run, she found her body was slowing down. Though her mind was still focused on her end goal, enough to push her forward, if she didn't get proper rest and nourishment soon, she wouldn't make it anywhere.

She removed the band from her hair and tried to run her hand through the tangles with a sigh. She really needed to take the time to run a brush through it thoroughly soon. With as long as she'd kept it and being on the run, it was impossible for it to not look like a rat's nest all the time. It would actually be best if she cut a good chunk of it off, maybe to her shoulders, so she'd blend in better. Deciding to worry about it later, she did her best to make it look as decent as possible before replacing the band. For the time being, she just wanted to keep her focus on staying safe and making sure she didn't get too comfortable.

If what Cade had told her was really true, she couldn't think of anywhere further removed from her previous life than a place meant to rehabilitate people who'd served in the military or in other law enforcement roles.

She kept her head down as she made her way back to the cafeteria, trying to go unnoticed by any of the new guests who had arrived. A few of them were at the front desk, presumably checking in, their attention on Hannah and her instructions. She quickly rushed by as Hannah's laughter filled the room.

River felt a pang of envy and longing when she heard it, and wondered if she would ever be able to laugh like that again. So carefree, with nothing to worry about, nothing to scare her, no reason to hide or be ready to flee from any danger that came her way.

She took a wrong turn coming out of the reception area and wound up in a corridor she didn't recognize. She stopped dead in her tracks and looked around. Where was she? She was about to turn around and retrace her steps when she heard a voice she recognized.

"Damn it," the voice muttered in frustration, and River glanced over at the door it was coming from. She slowly pushed it open and there, on the other side, was Cade. She felt a flood of relief when she saw him. She wasn't sure what it was about him, but there was something comforting about his presence, especially when she was as lost as she was.

As soon as he heard the door open, he looked up and put down the weights he had been holding. He was in what looked like a small gym area, with a handful of fitness machines lining the opposite wall and some free weights closer to the door. He grinned when he saw her, but when he noticed the look on her face, the smile soon faded to a frown.

"What's up?" he asked her. "Are you okay?"

"I—I'm fine," she replied, her voice giving her away. "I was just looking for the cafeteria, that's all. I guess I got turned around."

He eyed her for a moment, and the way he looked at her, it was as though he could tell there was something more going on inside her head than she wanted to admit. He took a step toward her and she felt her muscles tighten, her mind telling her to get ready to run.

She stood her ground. She didn't need to run. He wasn't going to do anything to her. If he was going to hurt her, he would have done it when he picked her up on the side of the road.

His pale gray eyes, the same color as the sky outside, looked at her with a mixture of wariness and concern like she was a wounded animal that could bite at any moment.

"Are you really all right, River?" he asked her softly.

There was something about the way he asked the question that made her stop dead in her tracks. It had been a long time since anyone had spoken to her with such gentleness and genuine caring, like he really gave a damn what her answer would be. She looked away from him quickly, swallowing down a rush of emotions that threatened to rise up and take over.

She didn't want to admit to him how long it had been since anyone had treated her with kindness, or even basic human decency. It wasn't his problem.

Sure, he seemed like he genuinely wanted to help her but she still wasn't going to tell him everything. He probably wouldn't even believe her if she stood there and told him the truth. It would sound ridiculous.

Feeling the tears sting her eyes, she blinked rapidly to clear them away and looked back up at him, plastering a smile on her face and hoping he couldn't tell how close she was to breaking down.

"Why do you care so much about some random hitch-hiker?" she demanded. She knew it was just a deflection tactic, but she didn't want to talk about herself right now, didn't want to admit how far from fine she was—and didn't want him to see how much his simple question had gotten under her skin. She needed to keep herself together.

And keep her eyes on the next part of her journey, instead of the man in front of her.

Chapter Five

Cade could tell River was on the brink of crying, and that just made him even more worried. Why would a simple question about how she was doing make her so emotional? Unless the truth was more horrible than she wanted to admit.

"You know, if you're in trouble, you should tell someone. I'm sure there's probably someone here who could help," he said gently.

Her jaw set tight and she lowered her gaze to the ground, clearly indicating the conversation was over. Cade tried to think of another way to approach the subject, not wanting to push too hard since she still looked like she might bolt at any moment. His mind came up blank, so he decided to change the subject altogether.

"You haven't eaten breakfast yet, right?" he asked her, picking up the weights again and moving them back over to the rack. Maybe it would be easier for her to talk about practical stuff, the physical rather than the emotional. She wouldn't be the first who had spent time here to feel that way.

"Not yet," she replied. "That's where I was heading, before I took a wrong turn."

"Let me clean up and I'll walk you down there," he told her. "And how did you sleep?"

"Okay, sure," she replied with a shrug, leaning up against the door.

She was still reluctant to tell him much more than the bare basics, and he could feel the anxiety coming off her in waves, but at least he could try and pull down some of those barriers she held on to so tightly. He wanted to know what was going on in her head, and why she seemed so nervous around everyone. It was clear she was afraid of something or someone and she wouldn't trust him with the whole truth of why she was on the road in the first place. Even though she was so secretive, he wouldn't have felt right about sending her back out on her own without at least trying to help in some way. Offer whatever assistance he could to make things a little easier for her while she was there.

"So, what exactly happens here?" she asked, tucking her hands behind herself and cocking her head at him. It was obvious she was just trying to get the attention off herself, but if she had questions, he was more than happy to answer.

"At the lodge?" he asked, and she nodded.

He shrugged a shoulder. "They have a variety of physical and mental rehab activities to help military and law enforcement deal with all kinds of injuries. That's why I'm here."

Her eyebrows shot up. "You got injured?"

"Yeah, former military. Got shot in the shoulder and my body banged up pretty good," he replied. "I've been working on getting back on my feet these last couple of years. And since my brother's been bugging me to come up for a while and he's one of the therapists, I thought I'd take him up on his offer and take advantage of the family discount at the same time and schedule some therapy."

He continued filling her in on his injury and his recovery, stopping short of coming clean about his doubts over his future. He didn't want to dump his problems on her. She wasn't asking about that part, and it seemed as though she had plenty to handle in her own right when it came to figuring out the future.

The way she reacted surprised him. Most people, when they heard about what he had been through, were instantly apologetic, trying to say the right thing and give him advice about what to do, but she just listened to him. He appreciated it more than he thought he would.

"…so yeah, that's what I'm doing here," he finished up and glanced over at her across the room. For the briefest moment, their eyes locked and the atmosphere in the room changed. Something about those big, blue eyes staring back at him made him stop in his tracks, and he felt something flicker in his chest—something he hadn't felt for a long time.

He could tell she felt it, too. She seemed to freeze for a moment, her eyes widening slightly, then her cheeks flushed a deep red and she tore her gaze away from his.

"Uh, um…" Her voice cracked. "I should go to breakfast, let you finish up. I'll find my way," she told him, ducking her head down and hurrying out of the gym before he could say anything else. He thought about going after her, but figured she needed her space.

Since River rushed out, he decided to continue what he'd started when she arrived. Once he'd finished his workout, he grabbed his bag and headed to the communal showers to get washed up, and then had breakfast. As he was re-filling his coffee thermos to head back down to the cabin where he was staying, Lawson appeared beside him, arms crossed over his chest.

"I heard you were here," he remarked.

Cade nodded at him in greeting. "Hey, Lawson."

"And that you brought someone with you," he continued. "Who's that woman you arrived with?"

Cade screwed the cap back on to his thermos before he replied. He should have known that Lawson was going to have questions about River, and he was probably right to. After all, he co-owned the place with Xavier, and he was Hannah's big brother. He had more reason than almost anyone to care about who came through those doors and what exactly their intentions were. And bringing in a mysterious stranger like River raised a whole lot of questions. As another former CIA agent, Lawson Davies was used to getting all the answers he wanted.

But before he could reply, Hannah bustled past, holding a nervous-looking River by the arm. Both men turned to watch as they passed, then Cade turned back to Lawson.

"I don't know much about her," he admitted. "I've been trying to get information from her, but she isn't giving much up."

"You should come in for a meeting with Xavier and me later today," Lawson told him firmly. "Three o'clock in the office. So we can talk. How long is she going to be staying here?"

"I don't know," Cade admitted.

"Well, one more day, and I'll want to talk to her myself," Lawson replied. "See if there's anything we can do to help her out."

"She doesn't talk much, trust me. I've tried." Cade shrugged as he looked after her down the hall where she and Hannah disappeared.

He wasn't sure what it was going to take to get her talking, or if she would ever be willing to open up at all. Maybe she just wanted to keep herself to herself, and do what he'd suggested—rest and refuel—then leave. Lawson was talking about her staying another day, but as far as Cade could tell, she was already ready to get back out on the road and continue on to wherever she was headed.

"Maybe she's in trouble with the law," Lawson suggested. "That's why she's keeping her mouth shut. Probably safer for her that way, huh?"

"I have no idea," Cade replied, but in his gut, he doubted it. She didn't strike him as the type who could cause any real trouble, but she might be caught up in some unwillingly. "She seems harmless, though."

Lawson clenched his jaw slightly. "Yeah, well, I'll be the judge of that," he replied.

"So, this meeting?" Cade inquired, directing the conversation away from River and her secrets. "Is something going on?"

"We want to run something by you, is all. Talk to you then, all right? I have to meet with a client." Lawson clapped him on the arm and then continued down the hall.

"Sure. I'll see you later," he told Lawson's retreating form, then turned to head out to his cabin.

Since Carter was with a patient that morning, Cade didn't have much more to do than wander around the grounds and get to know the area now that he was finally there. His brother had told him a little about the place when he had been trying to convince him to come. Cade was pretty sure the real reason Carter wanted him there was so he could keep a closer eye on him.

His brother knew better than anyone how hard Cade found it to just sit around and do nothing. When the two of them were growing up, they had always tried to outdo each other. From who could climb up the highest in the big oak tree in their backyard, to who could launch himself the furthest off the tire swing, and countless bicycle races down the driveway in between. Because of that, they frequently found themselves in the ER with their arms in a cast or their heads getting stitched up. It was why Carter had gotten interested in physical therapy in the first place, because he wanted to help people the same way he had been helped when he was a kid. Cade, however, had gone the other way entirely, craving the same kind of thrill they'd sought out when they were kids. That same adrenaline rush that lit a fire in his belly.

Cade found himself on a thin, gravel pathway that wound away from the main building. While most of the guests at the lodge stayed in the main building, there was a small cluster of cabins out in a clearing in the woods where people who were longer-term residents could stay. That was where Carter and some of the others lived and where he'd gotten Cade set up for his time there. He hadn't had much time to do anything other than drop his stuff off before grabbing a bite with the others and then crash on the bed the night before, but now that the rain had stopped, he wanted to get a better look at the place.

The path Cade was walking on cut through the dirt and a little bit of grass surrounding it, and led the way to the cabins. It was fall, and with the leaves beginning to change colors on the trees, it was really pretty out in the woods. This had always been Cade's favorite season, but it had been a while since he'd had a chance to spend it out somewhere rural like this. He sipped on his warm coffee as he followed the trail down to where he was staying, watching a few rays of sunshine peek through the gray clouds above him. Maybe it was going to be a nice day after all.

He reached the cabins surrounded by the low-lying branches of trees that sagged with red and gold leaves, and headed to his place. It wasn't much, but it was cozy enough, and exactly what he needed as long as he was there.

All the cabins were set back in the surrounding trees, like part of nature, and blended in perfectly with the forest. There were walkways leading up to the door of each unit. Each place had the same outside lighting, but they all had different interiors. The inside of his cabin was just slightly larger than the single units, with an open-floor concept in the front, then two small bedrooms separated by a tiny bathroom in back. The living area and kitchen were contained in the same space, the kitchen big enough to hold a small counter with two stools pushed underneath, a couple of cabinets, a compact sink and little fridge. A great place for a basic meal and cup of coffee if he didn't want to go up to the lodge. He liked the social aspects of the lodge, though, and he didn't want to miss out on it. Then there was the gym. He needed that space to get in his daily workout to keep in shape and help settle his mind in the midst of his recovery.

The living area was the larger of the two sections, and allowed for a couch, a small side table with a lamp, a comfy chair and a fireplace. Then the two bedrooms each with a queen-size bed, side table, dresser and small closet and then the shared bathroom.

Just before he reached his new home, he heard a laugh. Hannah's, if he wasn't mistaken. And then, it was followed by another female laugh he'd never heard before. He stopped in front of a cabin toward the end and peered inside, trying to get a look at what was going on in there.

That was when he saw it—Hannah and River together. But instead of the usual nervous, wide-eyed expression she had on her face, River was smiling. More than smiling, she was laughing. Her head was thrown back and her long hair flowed over her shoulders, her face lit up with joy. Her face was completely unguarded and she was beautiful.

Staring for a moment, Cade felt a smile spread over his own face. After how reserved and jumpy she had been, to see her smiling and laughing lifted a weight from his shoulders.

He found himself wondering what it would take for him to be able to get her to laugh like that.

Chapter Six

She had planned her day out in her mind as soon as she woke, before she had even left her room. She'd intended to scope out the area around the lodge, pick up as many supplies as she could and prepare to continue her journey as soon as she got the chance. But soon enough, she found herself running into Cade when she got lost, and then Hannah caught her before she could slip back off to her room.

"Oh, there you are!" she exclaimed, grabbing River by the arm as soon as she saw her. River had just eaten breakfast, a bagel with some bacon, and had been planning on heading back to her room to get started with her day. But as it turned out, Hannah had something else in mind.

"What are you up to today?" she asked, grinning widely at her. River tried to come up with some excuse, something to get away from her without seeming rude, but she couldn't think of anything.

"I was just going back to my cabin. You want to come check it out?" she suggested, and River found herself nodding before she could stop herself. Maybe she could use this opportunity to see a little more of the area this way, get a better idea of the layout of the property around the lodge. It would give her a reason to be seen wandering around if she was with Hannah, rather than possibly looking suspicious roaming around on her own.

Hannah led River down a gravel path away from the main building and toward the woods. River tensed as she followed her, and couldn't stop her eyes from darting around. It was going to be fine. Hannah wasn't going to hurt her. She had been nothing but kind and helpful since River arrived at the lodge. She took a deep breath to relax and reminded herself that not everyone was out to cause her harm.

Still, she kept her guard up as they reached Hannah's cabin, one seated in a cluster of them out in the woods. It was cute and simple with a couple of chairs out front and a little table in between them. A great place to sit and enjoy the sunrise before starting the day. The inside was basically one huge room with a small kitchen off to the side when you entered and what looked like a tiny bathroom in the back corner. It was also surprisingly colorful. Art hung on the walls, and photographs of Hannah with her friends and family were stuck all over a cork bulletin board next to the door. A huge, fuzzy orange carpet lay in front of the couch and bright pillows were tossed on the bed. The entire space matched her bubbly personality perfectly.

"I was just going to make myself a latte, you want one?" Hannah asked, gesturing to the large coffee machine that took up most of the space on her counter. River furrowed her brow.

"I've, uh, I've never had one," she admitted, blurting it out before she could stop herself.

Hannah stared at her for a moment, her eyes widening. "What do you mean, you've never had one?"

"I've just…not tried one yet," River mumbled, feeling her cheeks getting a little warm. She didn't want to seem weird or make her strange upbringing obvious, but she wasn't sure what else to say. She just hoped that Hannah didn't start asking questions that she didn't want to answer. River didn't want to make herself feel more uncomfortable by refusing to talk about her past. Thankfully, Hannah didn't press her for more.

"Oh, you have to let me make you one!" Hannah replied. "What flavors do you like? I have vanilla, hazelnut, pumpkin spice…"

A few minutes later, River held a steaming cup of what Hannah told her was a vanilla latte. It smelled sweet, the scent of it filling the cabin, as Hannah talked her ear off about her time at the lodge so far.

River used the opportunity to confirm that everything Cade had told her about the lodge was true. Everything he'd said checked out and she was relieved to learn that he hadn't lied to her. Maybe he really was just a nice guy who wanted to help her without any ulterior motives and make sure she was okay. She wouldn't let herself think too hard about why that made her so happy.

Hannah sighed, leaning a hip against the kitchen counter and taking a sip of her coffee. "It's so good to have Cade here. I know Carter has been trying to get him to come for a visit for a while now. It's also nice to have some new eye candy too. He is a mighty fine specimen."

"Oh, um, right," River replied awkwardly, not sure what she was supposed to say to that.

Hannah laughed. "Hey, don't get me wrong, I really like working with the other guys. They're nice to look at too, with the exception of my brother, of course. I see them every day, though. It's nice to have someone new around."

"Oh, your brother's here too?" River looked to Hannah for confirmation and she nodded before River continued on. "I briefly met Carter with you and I noticed him and Cade sitting with another man in the cafeteria last night, but I'm not sure who he was."

"Yeah, my brother Lawson owns the place with Xavier," Hannah replied softly, an emotion River couldn't quite place flitting through her eyes. It disappeared so quickly that River thought she might have imagined it. "Xavier was sitting at the table with Cade and Carter. I'm sure you'll meet them both while you're here."

Why did that comment suddenly make River nervous?

Before she could think of a response, Hannah's face turned playfully mischievous again and she pretended to fan herself. "But Cade...damn!"

River couldn't help but laugh at her antics. Though it was obvious Hannah was trying to get a response from her, she had such a bright, warm energy it was impossible not to be drawn to her.

Hannah leaned in, waggling her eyebrows. "I don't blame you one bit for getting in the vehicle with him, I totally would have too." River felt the heat in her cheeks burn a little darker, and hoped Hannah didn't notice. She would be lying if she said that she hadn't noticed how handsome Cade was. When she had run into him at the gym, the way his shirt plastered to his firm chest and the sweat glistening off his toned arms had made it hard to think straight. Then that sharp jawline, those gray eyes that seemed to cut right through her, there was no denying he was hot. It had been a long time since she'd actually felt an attraction to someone like that and it was both scary and exhilarating.

"So, I hope it's okay, but there's something I wanted to talk to you about," Hannah told her, cocking her head slightly. River's heart jumped in her chest, her panic returning. Had she figured her out? Was she going to ask her to leave? She swallowed hard and looked at Hannah, waiting for her to go on.

"I hope I'm not overstepping," she remarked, dropping her voice slightly. "But I…it's obvious that something's going on with you, River."

River stiffened, parting her lips, about to protest, but before she could say anything Hannah lifted a hand to stop her from speaking.

"And don't worry, I'm not going to try and make you tell me what it is," she promised her. "We all have a past, I get it. We don't have to get into it if you don't want to."

River breathed a sigh of relief. Even if she was getting a little more comfortable with Hannah, she wasn't going to let her guard down completely. She knew better than that.

"But if I were you, I'd take advantage of how much help we need around the lodge," she continued. "There's always stuff that needs to be done, and if you have any practical skills, there's a good chance you could put them to use here, get lodging and food for a while until you're ready to move on."

River wracked her brain, trying to come up with something useful she might be able to do. It wasn't as though she'd ever had a real job.

"Uh, I guess I… I can cook," she began. "And I can sew. I make clothes, actually."

"Oh, like the dress you were wearing when you arrived?" Hannah asked, and she nodded.

"I bet we could do something with that," she mused, tapping her finger on her chin. "There's always gear in the supply room that needs mending. I think Lawson spends a whole bunch of money on it every year. I could talk to them about it, if you want, see if there's a job here for you."

Hannah sounded so determined to help that River wasn't sure that saying no was an option. And maybe it *was* a good idea. If she was working here, she would be able to gather the supplies she needed to get out on the road again without attracting too much attention. It seemed safe enough, and having somewhere she could rest and recharge and focus on getting herself together again before she got back out on the road would be a good thing, right?

Plus, being around people who had combat history and seemed focused on their own recovery was probably going to make for a safer hiding spot than being out on the road ever would. She didn't like the thought of being in one place for too long. It made her feel itchy. It would also make it even easier for them to find her, but who would even think to look for her out here?

Besides, if she was really being honest with herself, she was so exhausted from all the running she had done. She needed time to clear her head and make sense of everything that had been going on, and come up with a solid plan for moving forward. She didn't have to stay forever, just a few weeks. She could get a little money and recharge, then turn her attention to getting back to her travels and finding her family once and for all.

"I guess it would be worth a shot," she replied.

Hannah clapped her hands together and pulled River into a tight hug. "Oh my God, you have no idea how happy I am to hear you say that."

River froze for a moment, not used to someone showing her affection, and then awkwardly returned the hug.

"It's been mostly guys here for way too long." Hannah went on, "We need another woman around the place. Right now, it's just Sarah, the on-site therapist, and myself. I'll talk to Lawson and Xavier as soon as possible, but I think they'll be glad to have someone else around here to help out."

"Thanks," River mumbled against her shoulder. She wasn't sure why Hannah seemed so intent on helping her, but she didn't appear to have any bad intentions, nor did she expect River to spill her life's story.

"There's a single cabin right next to mine," Hannah told her. "They're pretty small, as you can see, but they do the job, and you'll have your own bathroom so you don't have to share showers with the guys up at the lodge."

"Sounds nice," River replied, and she felt a smile spread over her face. She took a sip of the latte that Hannah had made for her, and its sweet warmth spread out over her tongue. She closed her eyes for a moment, savoring it. "Wow, that's really good," she remarked.

Hannah grinned. "You can have coffee with me every morning if you want to."

"I think I'd like that," River replied. She could feel something in her starting to relax and unwind from the tight coil it had been in since she had arrived here. Well, even longer than that if she was honest. Even if Hannah said it wasn't much, having a cabin to herself, something other than her shredded sleeping bag to rest in all night, would feel like the height of luxury to her.

She and Hannah spent the rest of the day together, with River tagging along as Hannah took care of her regular duties. Even though she didn't officially have a job here yet, Hannah insisted on showing her how things ran, and River was glad to have a look at this place from the inside out. The more she knew about how things worked, the safer she would feel. She appreciated any knowledge she could get on how to fit in at the lodge and not stick out like a sore thumb like she'd been doing since she got there. The first step would be to learn her way around so she didn't get lost again as she had that morning.

Hannah and River chatted as they walked back to Hannah's cabin once she was done with her responsibilities for the day. Well, Hannah did most of the talking, but River was glad for the company. Being on her own for so long, she hadn't exactly had a chance to get to know anyone in many years. It felt good to not be alone and to have someone to talk to about ordinary things.

"I'll see you tomorrow, all right?" Hannah told River, once they had reached her cabin. "I'll talk to the guys like I said, and I bet I can get them to agree to you staying here."

"Thanks, Hannah," River told her, and she really meant it. She didn't know why these people were being so kind to her, but she sure was thankful for it.

She made her way up the gravel path to the main entrance after saying goodbye to Hannah. Since it wasn't fully dark yet, she thought she might take the opportunity to do some more exploring around the outside of the lodge. She'd been inside with Hannah most of the day.

She walked in the direction opposite of the cluster of cabins, taking in the sight of the beautiful tress and enjoying the crisp air. The seasonal colors of fall highlighting the deep greens of the surrounding forest was a sight to behold. Off in the distance she heard a thumping sound and what sounded like animals—horses to be exact—milling around.

Curiosity got the better of her and she turned toward the noises, finding a trail that branched off from the one she was on. The whinnying of horses and a man's voice reached her ears right before the pathway opened up to a shelter-type area with a few horses trotting around a fenced-in area. A man she'd not seen before was hammering boards on the frame of the building. A handyman, maybe? Not wanting to interrupt or be caught somewhere she shouldn't be, she turned back to the main trail, deciding she'd ask Hannah or Cade about it later. She'd never ridden a horse before and wasn't sure she'd want to, but she would love to get a closer look at the beautiful creatures.

She realized she'd walked farther than she intended when she spotted another small building on the opposite side of the trail from where it branched off to the horses. She must have been so lost in thought on the walk out here that she hadn't even noticed it before. She wasn't going to pay attention to it now, but the light inside suddenly turned on and she could see the shadows of people moving around. She immediately felt unsettled and glanced around, making sure nobody was watching her. She needed to know who was in there, and she wouldn't be able to relax until she did.

As quietly as she could, River slipped over to the building, feeling her heart thrumming in her chest as she went.

She reached the door and pressed her ear to it. She heard

muffled voices—men, by the sound of it—coming from the other side. She pushed the door open slightly and peered around. A short distance inside, she could see men talking. River recognized a few of them—Cade, of course, and the couple of men who had been sitting with him in the cafeteria her first night. Xavier and Carter, maybe? Then there was another man she didn't think she recognized, but it was hard to tell because his back was facing her. And beside him, the sight of a man that made her stomach drop.

A cop stood right there, in the cluster of men. The hair on the back of her neck rose, and she felt a shiver run down her spine.

Chapter Seven

"So, what exactly is this about?" Cade asked as he looked around the group that had gathered in one of the small buildings behind the main lodge. Carter had walked out with him telling him that there would be someone else joining their meeting with Xavier and Lawson.

"Cade, this is Sheriff Willis," Lawson introduced the other man in the room.

The man extended his hand to Cade, and Cade took it, looking him up and down. He was a cop, no doubt about it.

"Good to meet you, sheriff." Cade nodded in greeting. "Now, is someone going to tell me what's going on here?"

"I've been hearing some rumors I thought you might be interested in." Willis replied, furrowing his brow. He brushed back a strand of his thinning gray hair, a concerned expression on his face.

"Rumors?" Cade asked, ears perking up. "About what?"

"We had a meeting with some other local law enforcement across state lines," he explained. "And all of us are seeing a marked uptick in gang activity. Not the usual kind, though, and that's what worries me."

"What's been going on?" Lawson asked, crossing his arms over his chest.

"All across the Carolinas, there's one group who's causing us a whole lot of headaches," he continued. "The Shepards of Rebellion."

Shepards of Rebellion. Cade repeated the name in his head, seeing if it stuck anywhere, but he couldn't place it at all.

"And what's this got to do with the lodge?" Xavier wondered aloud.

"We've been hearing stories of people getting robbed out on the Appalachian Trail, not far from you," he explained. "Figured you might want to let some of your guys know about it."

"People have been robbed? What for?" Carter asked, frowning.

"Weapons, mostly, but they've been taking other survivalist stuff too," Willis replied. "The Shepards, they don't seem like your normal gang, from everything we've seen. We can handle them making a little noise, starting a few bar fights, but this goes way beyond that."

"So, what have they been up to?" Cade demanded.

"Some dark stuff. Anarchist-type stuff," Willis remarked, shaking his head. "We're not sure how deep it goes, or exactly what they're planning, but they've got their tentacles across several states now, and it looks like they're going to try and keep expanding from there. You'll want to be on your guard. They've been on the Feds' radar for a couple of decades now, ever since they started back in Florida."

Florida? Cade's mind flashed to River at once. No way she had anything to do with that group, right? No, it was just a coincidence. She couldn't be involved in something like a dangerous gang. And besides, these gangs didn't exactly have people running around looking like cult members. They would try and keep their appearances as subtle as possible so they could blend in.

And there was no way River blended in anywhere she was in the world.

"Thanks, Willis," Xavier told the sheriff. "I appreciate you coming out here to let us know. If we hear anything about them, or notice anything suspicious around the lodge, we'll reach out to you, okay?"

"Sure thing," Willis replied. "Just keep your hikers off the trails for a while, make sure they know what they're dealing with. We don't want to cause a panic, but we don't want to give the Shepards any more victims to get their hands on, either."

"Of course," Xavier replied. "I'll walk you out," he gestured for the sheriff to follow him. "I've got to get back to the lodge anyway. Guys," he added with a chin lift before they walked out the door.

Cade watched until he was gone, and then turned back to the others.

"So, anything come up on those missing person reports?" he asked.

Lawson shook his head. "Nothing I could see outright," he replied. "Doesn't look like there's anyone out there looking for River, at least as far as I can tell with the little information we have on her."

Cade nodded, not sure if that was a good thing or not. Surely there had to be someone out there who had noticed she was gone? Someone who was searching for her. Whatever she was running from, it was clear she had reason to think it might catch up with her, and he didn't want to let anything get close to her.

"So, why exactly did you want me here for this meeting?" he asked, a little confused. He didn't work at the lodge. Just because his brother did and Cade was visiting, it surely didn't mean he had to be a part of these serious conversations with the cops.

Carter sighed, and then looked over to Lawson. "Go ahead."

Lawson turned to Cade with a serious expression. "Cade, there's something I'd like you to know about one of the things we do out here," he explained. "We run a tactical operations team out of the lodge. Well, mostly me. Xavier handles more of the day-to-day functions but he helps out when necessary."

Cade glanced between the guys, trying to figure out if this was some kind of joke, but they looked back at him with serious faces. He'd always thought something like this was going on up here in the background. No way could you get together so many people who had been involved in such demanding and all-consuming work and expect them to just forget about it while they focused on their recovery. They'd need to do some kind of physical activity, at least, for the missing adrenaline rush and to keep their skills sharp. So it didn't surprise him at all to find out that Lawson and Xavier, both being former CIA, had found a way to utilize those honed skills to help when necessary.

"And what exactly does that involve?" he asked.

"We work with law enforcement and other agencies in different capacities to help them take down any troublemakers in the area," he explained. "Usually, it's nothing too difficult, nothing too physical. A lot of it involves background research-type work, but it keeps us busy and makes sure the guys are keeping all areas of their skills current for when they want to get back into the field."

Cade cocked an eyebrow. "And you're telling me because…?"

"Because we want you to be part of it."

Cade felt a grin spread across his face. Of course that was what this was about. They knew as well as anyone how good he had been at his job, how seriously he had taken it. And even though his brother might have wanted him to keep his head down and focus on getting better, he was always going to be restless, searching for another way to use his skills.

He looked at each man in the room. "Just a reminder— I nearly got my skull split in two. Another injury, and I'll be out for good."

"We know," Lawson replied.

Carter bristled at Cade's words, and Cade knew his brother probably wasn't happy about this offer. But Carter knew better than to try to stop him; knew he'd go crazy without something to keep him busy.

Lawson continued. "Most of this work is surveillance-based, so you're not going to be in the line of fire. Backup to law enforcement is about as much action as you'll see. You shouldn't have to worry much about a reinjury. So, what do you think?"

Cade tapped his finger on his chin. It was a great offer, and something for him to stay active doing. He wanted to feel useful and to keep himself strong, physically and mentally. But he wasn't sure if he was ready for responsibility like this before he finished all his therapy. The last thing he'd want was to let them down or get himself or someone else hurt because he wasn't up to the job yet. At the same time, he'd never been one to back down from a challenge.

"I'll think about it," he replied to Lawson and held out his hand. "Thanks for the offer. It means a lot you'd consider me."

It was the best he could do right now. He didn't want to commit to anything without thinking it through. Even being asked to join the team was a boost to his ego, but he needed to be in the right headspace to consider the pros and cons of the role. He wanted to be useful again, to have a purpose that meant something and made a difference. This could be the opportunity he was looking for to prove to himself and others that he was capable.

Lawson dipped his chin and gave him a firm handshake. "Thanks for meeting with us."

Cade turned to leave, giving Carter a slap on the shoulder as he passed. He was sure they had some real work stuff to discuss, and he didn't need to stick around for that. He had never been as interested in the practical side of things—the day-to-day stuff—like running a business. Taking out bad guys was more his speed.

Besides, he was starting to get hungry.

He was just about to start down the path to the main lodge again, when he spotted someone hurrying away, like they didn't want to get caught.

He peered after the person's retreating form for a moment, and then he realized who it was—River. All that hair was a dead giveaway.

"Hey, River!" he called after her. Had she been eavesdropping on them? He couldn't imagine they were saying anything that might have interested her, but he didn't know for sure. And why was she trying to get away from him now that he had noticed her? It didn't make sense.

He took off after her and caught her arm just before she vanished back down the path to the woods once more. She spun around at once, and landed a sharp jab on his jaw, sending him reeling back in surprise.

"Damn!" he exclaimed, rubbing his jaw. She stared up at him, her eyes wide, her face pale.

"I'm sorry," she blurted out.

He shook his head in disbelief. "Where did you learn to hit like that?" he asked.

She was so slight, almost fragile, it was hard to believe she could hit that hard.

"Street fighting," she replied, and he couldn't tell if she was joking or not. There was a lot about her that was hard to read, but he got the feeling that was by design. She didn't want anyone getting too close, finding out too much about her. But she could only get away with that for so long before she would have to tell them at least something about her past and what she was running from, especially if she wanted to stay. Lawson wouldn't have it any other way. It was his and Xavier's responsibility to make sure this place was safe for their guests. If either of them thought she was a threat in any way, they'd surely ask her to leave.

She wrapped her arms around herself protectively, her eyes lowering to the ground.

Cade stared at her. He still didn't know what was going on with this woman or how to get by her walls, but he wanted to help her if he could. If she'd just meet him half-way and open up some...

He decided to try again, "River, please tell me what's going on with you."

She shook her head and held herself tighter. "It doesn't matter."

"Yes, it does," he replied gently, trying to keep his voice as patient as he could. "I know you're going through something. It's obvious. I just want to help you..."

He trailed off with a weighted sigh. He could immediately tell this approach was not working, again.

Stubborn woman. She obviously didn't want anyone's help. Or maybe she didn't believe that anyone would want to help her. He wasn't sure if there was anything he could say or do that would convince her to trust him, even a little. Well, he could be stubborn too and he was damn sure going to try to change her mind.

Cade watched her hug herself tighter and she still wouldn't meet his eyes. He decided to try a more direct approach and hope that didn't scare her off for good. "If you're going to stay here, then you're going to need to open up a little. Give us a little background on yourself."

No matter what had happened to her, he was sure there were plenty of people out there who had been through the same. Nobody suffered in a way that was exclusive to them, he had learned that in his recovery.

She paused for a moment, going completely still. Cade could almost see the wheels turning in her brain, clearly trying to decide how much she should tell him. What she could trust him with. Cade tensed and held his breath in anticipation. Then something seemed to shift inside of her.

He saw it when her eyes lifted to his. It was like she finally realized that she couldn't keep all of her secrets hidden.

She let out a resigned breath. "I was going to have to get married to someone I didn't want to marry. It wasn't a good situation," she replied, not making eye contact again. "So, I left."

And just like that, Cade felt some of the barrier she held between them come down and his body somewhat relaxed at her confession. It wasn't much, but it was a start, and right now he would take what little bit he could.

Chapter Eight

She stood there pushing the toe of her shoe around in the gravel and staring up at Cade, wondering if she had just made a huge mistake in giving him even that much information.

Maybe she should have told him it was none of his business, but how long was that going to work before they asked her to leave? How long was she going to be able to keep the truth hidden?

Besides, she knew they were taking a big risk by letting a stranger whom he'd picked up on the side of the road stay at the lodge. They had to protect themselves and their guests from whatever trouble someone like her could bring to their door.

Better to give Cade a little than have him go looking for it himself and dig up the reality of what she had left behind. They all knew something was going on with her, and her appearance when she arrived spoke volumes on its own.

"You were going to marry someone?" he asked. He looked a little confused, and she couldn't blame him. After all she had been through, sometimes she still had a hard time believing any of it was actually real. It seemed like it had come from a different reality, a reality she never wanted to be anywhere near again as long as she lived. But she knew she wasn't going to be able to hold that reality at a distance much longer. She had been through a whole hell of a lot, and at some point, she was going to have to admit it to herself. And deal with it before the past caught up with her.

"Yeah," she replied, kicking at a bit of dirt on the ground to distract herself from the conversation.

"Seems like you've gone to great lengths to get away from this person," he observed. "You said you came from Florida, right?"

"I wanted to make sure there was plenty of distance between us," she replied. "I…he's not the kind of guy who gives up easily. Especially when he thinks he's owed something."

She knew she shouldn't say too much, but there was something about Cade that made her want to trust him.

"Owed something…? Was he violent with you?" Cade asked.

She nodded.

Anger flashed in his eyes but his voice came out controlled. "I'm sorry," he told her sincerely.

She shrugged. "It's fine," she replied. "I… I'm away from him now, that's all that matters."

"Was there any reason you didn't try to take a plane or train to get away from him?" Cade asked.

She sighed. "He didn't exactly leave me with any money of my own," she admitted. "And besides, he's the kind of guy…if he wanted to track me down, he could. If someone saw me on public transport, it would get back to him, and he would find me. I'm sure of it."

She pressed her lips together tightly and shivered at the thought. Even imagining him within ten feet of her made her want to vomit. She tried to remind herself how far she had come, how much distance she had managed to put between them. It wasn't enough, though. Not even close. She wasn't sure if it was ever going to be enough.

Cade nodded grimly. "I see."

She wasn't sure he really did. She could see him processing everything she'd told him as he stood there in front of her, a multitude of emotions flashing through his eyes.

Finally, his eyes met hers. "Then you're staying here," he said in a tone that brooked no argument.

She felt a wave of relief pass through her. Even though Hannah had all but made that decision for her, having the guys on her side—especially Cade—would only make things easier. For a moment, she thought about telling him about her plans to get to her sister, to find her family in New York, but the less anyone knew about her family, the better.

"I think Hannah already decided that," she remarked with a small smile.

He started walking in the direction of the lodge. "Yeah, she likes to have things her way," he replied with a low chuckle.

River caught up with him, falling in line with his pace. She felt more of her tension leaving her body as they walked down the path. Now that she had told him a little bit of her story, it was like a weight had lifted from her shoulders. She didn't have to worry anymore about him finding out what was going on behind the wall she had put up between herself and the rest of the world.

"I think I'm starting to find that out," she replied in a brighter tone. "Has she been working here a long time?"

"She's Lawson's little sister, so I think she's been here since the start," he replied, as he held the door to the main lodge open for her.

She brushed past him, and caught the scent of his aftershave for a split second—something deep and woodsy and masculine that filled her senses and made her head spin. She forced herself to keep walking, even though all she wanted was to press her face into his neck and breathe it in. She could feel her cheeks burning, and she tried to shut down that embarrassing line of thought. She needed to remember why she was in her current situation. She definitely would *not* be jumping into something—relationship or otherwise—with another man anytime soon. Even one who seemed as nice as Cade.

Before she could think on it any longer, Hannah called her name from the other side of the reception desk. She stood there with a familiar-looking man, who had a slightly bemused expression on his face. Cade and River walked over to where they stood.

"So, I was just telling Xavier... You've met, right?" Hannah asked, looking between the two of them.

River turned her attention toward the man, Xavier, who replied, "No, not officially. Nice to meet you, River."

"Hello. You, too," she replied politely, though her stomach was suddenly in knots.

"Anyway," Hannah continued. "I was telling Xavier about your skills with clothes. That you could sew, right?" She eyed River for confirmation.

River suddenly felt the words catch at the back of her

throat. Xavier turned to her expectantly. Panic seized her and she swallowed heavily, trying to pull herself together. She knew she needed to make herself useful if she was going to convince them to let her stay, but a small part of her still didn't know if she should trust them.

"Uh, yeah, I can sew," she answered in a small voice, darting her gaze between them, then lowering her eyes to the ground. It was something she'd learned the hard way a long time ago, avoiding eye contact, especially with men, so it didn't look like they were being challenged in some way. Make herself seem smaller, meeker, more submissive.

"Well, we do need someone to mend up the gear and catalog everything we've got," Xavier remarked. "But we can't hire you without ID. Are you willing to provide that?"

She tensed up. She couldn't. She couldn't give them any more information than they already had. What would happen if they found out too much and wanted to hand her over to the cops—or worse, to him? She tried to find the words to tell him she couldn't do that, but under the scrutiny of his gaze, she couldn't seem to muster the courage to tell him no.

All at once, she felt Cade step behind her, the comforting weight of his presence at her back helping to calm her so she could think straight.

"Domestic dispute with an ex, Xavier," he told the other man. "And she's trying not to be found."

Xavier eyed her for a long moment, and River couldn't bear to look up at him. She was glad she had told Cade the little that she had, so he could share what she couldn't. It was nice to finally have someone on her side, or she might have run and never looked back.

To her surprise Xavier nodded decidedly. "Then you can stay," he said simply. "We'll pay you under the table. Nobody has to know you're here."

River breathed a sigh of relief and leaned lightly back into Cade. She opened her mouth to thank him, but he continued before she got any words out.

"On the condition that you take advantage of the facilities we have here," he went on. "Therapy. Anything else you need. And when you're ready to go public with it, we'll be here for you. Okay?"

She was speechless for a moment and she couldn't help the tears of gratitude that gathered in her eyes. It was more than she could ever hope for. They believed her. They were letting her stay. She hadn't felt this safe or comfortable in a long time. And maybe if she had the chance to work and take advantage of the counseling and other resources offered at the lodge, it would help her find her footing and allow her a chance to mentally heal.

She nodded, finally returning her gaze to his. "Okay. Thank you, Xavier."

Hannah clapped her hands together. "This is awesome!" she exclaimed. "I'll help you move your stuff down from your room to your cabin later, if you want."

"Cade, can you show River the supply room?" Xavier asked.

"Sure thing," Cade replied.

She turned to him with a bright smile on her face. She wasn't sure she was ever going to be able to communicate to him just how grateful she was for how he'd helped her. But she was going to do her best to pull her own weight and be as helpful as possible. She might not have a lot of useful skills, but she would do what she could to the best of her ability.

She followed Cade to the supply room, which turned out to be more of a supply basement. It was filled with seasonal clothes, equipment and other stuff that would have made it all too easy for her to swipe stuff and take off again if she wanted. The thought crossed her mind as she looked around the room, but when she glanced back at Cade, she felt a twist of guilt for even considering it. After all the kindness he'd shown her, she couldn't do that to him. She quickly pushed the thought out of her mind and turned her attention back to him.

He gestured to the scattered mess in front of them. "I know it's a lot to sort out, but Hannah'll be able to point you in the right direction on where to start," he said. "I've been here as long as you have and I still have a lot to learn."

"Right," she agreed, and she slipped her hands into her pockets as she looked around the room more. She felt Cade watching her, and she turned around to see him staring at her intently. Judging by the expression on his face, there was something bothering him.

"What is it? Are you okay?" she asked, worried. She took a step toward him, trying to gauge his emotions and what might've disturbed him. She was used to being highly attuned to the emotions of everyone around her. She knew it was a defense mechanism she had learned to protect herself. Even though she had no reason to think Cade was going to treat her the way she'd been treated by others in the past, it still made her nervous.

He gazed down at her for a moment and the air in the room grew taut, those striking gray eyes on hers, and she felt her breath catch. She wasn't sure what was on his mind, but she wished she could figure it out. The longer she was trapped in his gaze, the more unsettled she felt.

"Yes, I'm fine," he replied. "I'll leave you to it." He looked at her for another moment, almost like he was committing her face to memory, and then turned to the door.

River stared after him, her heart in her throat as she tried to figure out what had just happened and what she should do next. What if being here was putting these people in more danger? What if someone got hurt because of her? She was glad she had someplace to stay for a while, but her mind suddenly drifted back to that building and the meeting the men had with that cop. She hadn't been able to make out anything being said, but what if it had been about her? Or worse yet, *him*? Guilt suddenly settled heavily in her stomach.

But she didn't have any other options right now, no choice but to stay put and hope she was safe here. Maybe she would tell them the truth at some point down the line after she was more familiar with everyone. When she knew for sure she could trust them.

Or maybe she would keep the rest of her past to herself in hopes she wouldn't be tracked this far. Not knowing for sure, it would be better not to share more than she had to Cade. Safer for everyone around. It would save them from being aware of the horrors she'd already survived.

Chapter Nine

"You're really thinking about joining Lawson's crew?" Carter asked as he guided Cade's knee back to his chest to test his mobility. Cade sighed. He should have known this physical therapy session was going to turn into an interrogation when Carter had offered it that morning. He had hoped everything that had been going on with River and the news of the Shepards of Rebellion being in the area would keep his brother distracted.

Cade shrugged. "It'll give me something to do."

Carter shook his head. Cade was currently laid out on his brother's therapy table like an offering of some kind, being tortured physically—with different stretches and movement rotations to test his flexibility—while also forced to endure Carter's questions. He'd rather be doing almost anything than this.

Carter narrowed his eyes. "You have plenty to do," he reminded him. "You've got to focus on your recovery, remember? That's what's important right now."

"Yeah, well, I need something to work toward," Cade replied. "This'll do me good. And Lawson knows what my limitations are. He's not going to try and push me into anything I can't handle."

Carter looked doubtful. "Yeah, I'll believe that when I see it."

"Are we done here?" Cade asked a little impatiently. He knew his brother was just trying to help, but he didn't want to deal with his questions and concerns right now. Carter should know better than anyone how much he needed to keep himself busy because he was the exact same way.

Carter nodded. "Let's get in another session this week."

Cade agreed and headed out the door to go grab some coffee in the cafeteria, but he was stopped by Hannah in the lobby.

"Hey, Cade, have you got a minute?" she asked.

"Sure," Cade replied. He could already guess this had something to do with River. It seemed to be all anyone could talk about since they had officially decided to keep her around.

"I was talking to Lawson this morning about getting River moved into one of the empty cabins," she explained. "And he doesn't want her…rooming alone, if he can avoid it."

Cade bristled slightly. What did this have to do with him? And why was Hannah suddenly not looking at him? He'd just opened his mouth to ask but snapped it closed as she continued.

"They've got some guys coming in for a conference in the next week or so, and all the rooms will be full. They're also going to spill over into a couple of the cabins, and he wants to keep the others free for any emergencies that might pop up with the lodge being at capacity," she continued. "So, um, Lawson asked if…she can bunk with you for the time being."

Cade stared at her. "He wants her to stay with me?" he asked. "If he's just trying to cut down on the cabin space being used, wouldn't it make more sense for her to bunk with you? I feel like she might be more comfortable with that. Since you're both women..."

He left the rest of that sentence hanging and continued to watch Hannah squirm under his scrutiny, pursing her lips. He could suddenly tell from the look on her face that this request was about more than saving space.

"Lawson wants me to keep an eye on River. That's what you're not saying, right?"

At the shift in her posture and widening eyes, Cade knew he had guessed right. It wasn't exactly ideal and he didn't really like it, but he understood the reasoning behind it. Since River was going to be with them long-term and he had brought her to the lodge in the first place, Lawson wanted him to be the one to watch her to make sure she wasn't causing trouble or doing anything she shouldn't be.

Hannah ignored his questions. "She only had her backpack and I've already taken that down to your cabin," she quickly continued. "She's getting breakfast now and I mentioned to her that you needed to chat with her and would find her there. So, she should be waiting for you. And I thought you could walk her over after you got through talking so she could get settled."

"You're leaving it up to me to tell her? Hannah, I don't think..."

"You'll do just fine, Cade. The guys do want to help her and I want her to stay. I love the idea of having another woman around to talk to. She seems closest to you, though, and we thought this would be easiest coming from you." Hannah patted his arm and turned away with a smile.

Cade released a heavy sigh. This was not going to go well. She was on the run from an abusive ex, and now she was going to be stuck bunking with a guy she barely knew? He couldn't imagine she would be very happy about it. But they would have to find a way to work it out, no matter how inconvenient it was for both of them.

Cade debated on going straight to the cafeteria, but decided he needed a minute to collect his thoughts. He headed down to his cabin, and sure enough, her backpack was already sitting on the couch when he got there. He stared at it for a moment, fighting the urge to go through it and see what else he could find out about her. Now that they were up close and personal and staying in the same cabin, he guessed he was going to be finding out more about her than he had ever imagined he would. Whether that was a good thing or not remained to be seen.

Before he could do anything with her bag, his phone buzzed—a message from Xavier asking him to come up to the lodge so they could talk.

Was he going to get a break today? He guessed this was what he'd wanted when he had come to the lodge in the first place…a chance to actually keep himself busy instead of sitting around on his ass doing nothing. He redirected his route to meet with Xavier first since his conversation with River would probably be more involved. Cade rapped his knuckles on the open doorframe before stepping farther into Xavier's office, and saw him seated behind his desk working.

"Ah, there you are," Xavier greeted him, closing his laptop. "I've got a job for you."

"Okay, what's up?" Cade asked, sinking down into the chair opposite him. Anything that would keep him out of the cabin and allow him a little space after he spoke to River was a welcome distraction.

"We need someone to head down to Blue Ridge and pick up some supplies," he said, pulling a credit card from the drawer beside him and pushing it and a printed list across the desk to Cade. "Here. Use this. It's the one we use for all the expenses tied to the lodge."

"Sure thing." Cade scanned the list, then pocketed it and the card as he stood.

Xavier lifted a hand to stop him. "One more thing," he added. "Take River with you."

"What?" Cade jolted slightly at the request. "Why? Isn't she working on the clothes?"

"Yeah, but some of the supplies we need are for her, along with the food list I gave you," he replied. "We don't want people going down to the town alone anymore, not after everything Willis told us."

"You think there could be trouble out there?" Cade asked, shoulders tensing slightly.

"We don't know, but we're not sending people out alone for the foreseeable future," Xavier replied. "Groups of two or three until further notice. And River will know what she needs for the mending, so she'll be best suited to go down there with you today. Maybe you can also help her pick up some items for herself while you're down there. And keep an eye out."

"All right, yeah, sounds good," Cade replied. If it was

what it took to keep the rest of the team feeling safe, he would do it. And besides, maybe it would give him a chance to get River's thoughts on them sharing a cabin. Spending time together was something they were going to have to get used to, now that they were living under the same roof.

He wandered through the lodge until he spotted her in the cafeteria. She wore the same dress she'd had on the first time he'd seen her on the side of the road, but it had been cleaned, so it looked like new. The skirt nearly brushed the floor, and the sleeves fluttered over her slim arms. Her hair was loose around her shoulders, held away from her face with a couple of clips as she filled up a thermos with tea. For a moment, Cade just stood there and looked at her. She was beautiful.

He didn't want to shout across the room, so he walked toward her and waited until he was next to her to say her name. When he did, she jumped so hard she nearly spilled her tea.

"Oh my gosh!" she exclaimed, spinning around to face him. "Don't sneak up on me like that!"

"I'm sorry," he apologized. "I spent too long in the army. I'm used to making a quiet approach."

She looked up at him, her eyes wide, and he could see her chest rising and falling rapidly with each breath. She was genuinely terrified. He could only imagine what she had been through with her ex. He was determined to show her she had nothing to fear when it came to him.

"How about I start wearing a bell?" he joked. "That way, you'll always hear me coming."

She let out a giggle and brushed a strand of hair back behind her ear. The way her fingers skimmed across her skin was far too distracting, but he did his best to push that out of his mind. He was here for a reason, not just to check her out. Xavier had asked him to do a job and he was going to be as helpful as he could during his stay at the lodge.

"Sounds like a plan to me," she replied with a small smile. "Hannah said you needed to talk to me. Do you want to go sit?"

He grinned back at her and shook his head, then held up the credit card he'd been given.

"Actually, I've been tasked with heading down to the town to pick up some supplies," he explained. "And they want us to start going in groups, so I'm supposed to take you with me. I thought we could talk on the way."

Her face lit up. "Oh, great," she replied as she reached into her pocket. "I actually have a list of stuff I need to get so I can work on mending clothes and stock up on supplies." She held the list out to Cade. "You think we'll be able to get all of this stuff in town?"

"I think so," he replied, taking it from her and looking it over.

It looked pretty easy to him, nothing too extreme—basic fabrics and a few glues and needles to make her work a little easier. He was a little surprised that she seemed so eager to go to town with him, given how nervous she had been about being seen outside this place. Maybe she was beginning to feel more comfortable and had realized that nobody would come looking for her in a place like this.

She screwed the cap onto her thermos and smiled up at him. "Then we should get going before it gets too late."

She had the prettiest smile when she let herself relax and Cade was mesmerized. He was really glad to see she was starting to let her guard down, especially with him. Maybe this was the start of a healing journey for her, just like Blue Ridge had been for so many others. There was still a long way for her to go, but even the small change he'd seen in her since yesterday felt huge.

"Great. I'll bring the truck around," he told her. "Meet me outside the front entrance in five minutes?"

"I will," she replied, and she gazed up at him for a moment like she was trying to puzzle something out.

For a split second, Cade was rooted to the spot, looking back at her.

But then, he remembered they were not alone and he had a job to do. He quickly broke the eye contact and turned to go get the truck. She had just gotten out of an abusive relationship. The last thing she needed was him drooling over her like a hormonal teenage boy.

He was trying to help this woman, that was it.

That was all it could be.

He had his own life to sort out.

Chapter Ten

River rolled down the window as they pulled away from the lodge. It was a cool, clear day, the sky was blue above them, and the air smelled fresh and clean from the recent rain. She stuck her hand out of the opening and swam it in the air as they made their way down the winding road that led to the town at the bottom of the mountain. A smile spread over her face as she tipped it up toward the sun.

Even though her time at the lodge was just beginning, she was starting to actually believe she had something good here. A safe place to stay, new friends, a job of her own where she'd make her own money. It almost felt like a dream.

"You sleep well?" His voice suddenly broke their peaceful ride.

She glanced toward him and nodded. "Actually, I did."

It was the truth. For the first time in a while, she had actually slept through the night instead of jumping up every five minutes to check that nobody was following her or she wasn't being watched. And she had actually slept in the bed instead of sitting on the edge of it, dozing off clutching her knife in her hand. She wasn't sure how much longer this newfound confidence was going to last, but she wanted to enjoy every moment of it while she could.

"Good, that's good," he murmured, and she glanced over at him. He had one arm leaning on the window, and his eyes on the road, but she could tell his attention was on her. "Speaking of that, there's something we need to discuss. I actually just found out this morning."

River couldn't help but tense a little at his odd-sounding tone and clench her fingers in her lap. Did something happen concerning her? She wasn't sure she wanted to know, but the mood in the truck suddenly shifted. Instead of asking, she waited silently for Cade to continue.

"So, apparently, there's going to be some sort of event happening at the lodge and it's booked out to capacity." He cleared his throat and shifted in his seat, suddenly nervous. "I, ah, was told that we're going to be sharing my cabin for a while."

"Oh." River couldn't help the anxious energy that washed over her at his words. She wasn't sure what else to say. She was hoping to have her own space and sharing with Cade certainly wasn't ideal—but she didn't mind too much. She was really curious what he thought of them sharing space but she wasn't sure how to approach the subject.

"Yeah, ah, Hannah brought your backpack over this morning and thought it'd be easier if we discussed it rather than having a go-between." He turned to look at her for a moment before concentrating back on the road. "If it's really uncomfortable for you, I'm sure Xavier can work something else out. She mentioned them holding a couple of other cabins for overfills, but I'm sure they'd consider one for you if it was an issue…"

He sounded about as nervous as she felt. She didn't know if it was because he didn't want to room with her or if it was something else. "So, roommates, then." River darted another glance in his direction before looking down at her lap. So much for her newfound confidence. She was out of her league here. The thought of being alone with this man… No, she wasn't going there. She'd find a way to make do. Stay away from the cabin as much as possible, if she had to. "I'm sorry to inconvenience you like this. I'll try to be as quiet as possible. You won't even know I'm there."

"I don't know about that," she heard him mutter under his breath. Clearing his throat he replied, "Don't worry about it. I just hope it's not too uncomfortable for you, what with me basically being a stranger and all. I promise you're safe with me, though." River felt a rush a warmth spread through her body as Cade's steady gaze shifted again to her before turning back to the road.

"You think we'll be able to find what I need in town?" she asked again, trying to change the subject to a safer topic.

She still wasn't totally sure about showing her face in Blue Ridge, but with Cade there as well, at least she had someone she could hide behind. It was hard to believe anyone would think to look for her here, and she just had to hope the locals weren't interested in who she was or why she had showed up there out of the blue.

"I think so," he replied with a nod. "A lot of people around here take care of their own clothes like you do. There's a craft store that sells pretty much everything you could need."

"You know this place pretty well, then?" she asked, and he nodded.

"Yeah, I stayed here for a while before I moved up to the lodge," he explained. "I started off in the city when I was recovering, but I came down here to be closer to my brother and his work."

"What's it like?" she asked curiously.

"Well, everyone knows everyone," he said with a smile. "At least, during the off season. In the summer, they get a lot of tourists through here, which is how the town makes most of its money. Mostly hikers looking to hit the trails. But the rest of the time, it's pretty quiet."

He filled her in on the town a little more, and she nodded as she took it in, watching the road outside as it wound down into the town. She hadn't had a good look at it the first time she had been out here, but it was really pretty in the sunlight. The leaves on the trees that lined the road were turning gold and red and brown, and a few floated down on to the road as they drove.

They reached the outskirts of the town, which wasn't much more than a few streets wrapped around a small central square. Cade pulled the truck to a stop next to the square, which was framed by perfectly manicured bushes on each side. He climbed out and rounded the hood, and this time, she allowed him to open the door for her instead of flinging it off its hinges herself. He offered her a hand to jump out, and she slipped her fingers onto his palm for a moment.

There was something about touching him that seemed to make the whole world slow down around her for a split second, something she couldn't quite put into words. He smiled at her, and she just looked at him, the moment freezing and burning itself into her head.

She hopped out of the truck and forced her mind back to reality. It was nothing. It was such a long time since she had actually felt safe with someone. That's why she was reacting this way to him. She wasn't falling for him or anything. She wasn't even sure she would know what that felt like, if she was being honest. She could admit, though, that she did enjoy having him around. If it wasn't for him, she would probably be out on the freezing roads again, trying her luck with whatever driver would pull over and pick her up.

"The craft store's just over there," he said, pointing down the street to a quaint little shop called Thread the Needle with seasonal decorations in the window—pumpkins with carved-out faces, plastic skeletons and fake cobwebs dangling from every corner.

"I have a few errands to run afterward, so maybe we can explore some more?" he suggested.

She nodded. "I'd really like that. I'd like to see about getting a few things for myself, if possible. Xavier gave me a little advance to grab some stuff."

He held the door open when they got to the store. A bell over the door announced their arrival, and an older woman behind the counter looked up and smiled when she saw them come in.

"Oh, hello there, Cade! It's been a while," she greeted them brightly. "And who's this? I don't think we've met, sweetie."

"This is River. We've come down from the lodge to get some supplies," Cade said, hooking a thumb in her direction.

River lifted her hand in an awkward wave and gave the woman a small smile that she hoped didn't look too nervous.

The woman's eyes darted over her dress, taking it in. "I'm Mary. Mary Cinder." After introducing herself, she stepped around the counter and planted her hands on her hips. "Did you make that dress yourself?" she asked.

River tensed, but nodded.

"It's wonderful," she said, shaking her head as she looked it up and down. "Totally unique. I love the design you've used for the bodice and the sleeves…so rare for a young woman like you to take an interest in sewing like that."

"Thank you," she replied softly, smiling bigger this time.

It had been a long time since anyone had complimented anything she had done, and she would be lying if she said it didn't feel a little strange. But the woman, Mary, seemed totally sincere, so she tried to brush off the doubts in the back of her mind.

"Of course, dear," Mary replied. "It's a lost art, and it's people like you who are going to keep it alive for the next generation. Do you quilt, too?"

"Um, I've done a little in the past, but not much."

"You should join our quilting group," Mary told her firmly, as though she wasn't going to take no for an answer. "We meet bimonthly, it's a lovely group of ladies. I bet you could teach them a thing or two, based on this dress, anyway."

"Oh, I don't know about that."

"Do you mind if I take a closer look at your stitching on the collar?" Mary asked, taking a step toward River. River hesitated for a moment, not sure if this was a good idea, but she forced herself to nod.

"Sure. Go ahead," she replied, and Mary examined the back of her dress, chatting away to her about the skills she'd have needed to make it. River didn't tell her the truth of how she'd learned those skills—their necessity for survival—but she appreciated her kindness.

"Give me your list, River, and I'll start getting the stuff while you ladies chat." Cade made his way around the store, picking up everything on her list, and by the time Mary was done looking at her dress, he was ready to check out.

"Thank you for coming," Mary said on their way out the door. "River, hon, please keep in mind about the quilting. I'd love to see you again."

"I will. Thanks," River gripped the bag of supplies as she and Cade left the shop.

Once outside, he led her to the next shop, which looked like some sort of ladies' store where she could get a few items of clothing and personal things.

"You think you can make me a new winter jacket?" he asked as he took the bag from her hand when they entered. "Sounds like you really know what you're doing, if you've got Mary that impressed."

"I could try," she replied. "But fair warning, my favorite color to work with is pink."

He chuckled. "Hey, I've been told it looks good on me," he teased. "Besides, if you made it, I'd wear it with pride. A River original, right?"

She blushed slightly and grinned at him. She felt lighter than she had in a long time, even though she knew she should have been nervous, being out in public like this.

But with Cade, it was as though nothing bad could happen to her—nothing could even come close.

They made their way around the town, picking up everything Xavier had asked him to get. He even introduced her to a few of the people he knew from his time living here. They all seemed happy to see him. A good sign, right? People liked him. He had clearly made a good impression on them when he had been staying in town, and they all treated her like an old friend because of him.

They grabbed lunch at a little place not far from the square. It was just a tiny hole-in-the-wall café, but after so long on the road having to live on whatever scraps she could find, it all tasted like gourmet food to River. She ate her toasted sandwich and soup like she had never seen food before in her life. She was still getting used to having three meals a day, her body recuperating all the lost calories from her previous lack of meals.

"Good?" Cade asked.

She nodded, holding her hand over her mouth to avoid showing him her mouthful of food. "Really good," she replied once she had swallowed the delicious bite.

"I'm glad." Cade chuckled.

He had a slightly crooked smile, but it lit up his whole face every time, as though he was genuinely glad to be with her. She felt that flutter in her chest again, and did her best to ignore it.

It wasn't until their drive back up to the lodge with the supplies that it hit her—she hadn't thought about leaving today. Not once.

It was all thanks to Cade. He made her feel so comfortable in a way she hadn't in a long time—maybe ever. That was making it more difficult to think about walking away when the time came. But if he knew who she really was and what she was running from, she was sure he would feel differently about her and her being at the lodge.

But she wasn't going to tell him more than she needed to. He made her feel safe, but she was going to keep her mouth shut and focus on taking care of herself. She wasn't going to get too settled into the lodge's atmosphere. It was way too dangerous to do that.

"You okay?" Cade asked.

She nodded and forced herself to smile. "I'm fine," she replied. "Thanks for bringing me with you and helping me get everything today."

"No problem," he replied. "You need any help getting your stuff out to our cabin?"

Our cabin. It was strange for him to say it like that. She supposed it was the right way to talk about it, but it still threw her a little hearing it. Staying with him was going to make it harder to steal supplies if she needed to run again, but she'd figure that out when and if the time came.

"No, I'm fine. I just had my backpack in my room and then what I got today," she replied once the truck had pulled up at the lodge again. She jumped out of her side, not waiting for him this time.

"I need to run these supplies inside and check in with Xavier before heading to the cabin," he volunteered as he turned off the engine and started gathering bags to haul inside the lodge. "You want me to take the sewing stuff with me?"

"That's okay, I'll take it with me and then just bring it up to the lodge tomorrow," she replied as she turned and headed to the cabin they were going to be sharing for the next little while.

"I'll be down in a bit after I get all this settled, then," he replied and she gave him a little wave as he walked away.

She'd have to work on getting used to having him around, in the same space. She'd been on her own for so long now, she wasn't used to other people being so close. Especially someone like Cade.

Luckily his cabin had a second bedroom, so when she got inside, she went straight to it and closed the door behind her. She just needed a few minutes on her own, to decompress and settle her mind. Her head was a mess as she thought about how she was going to handle him, but she didn't want to lose the flutter in her chest when he was around.

No matter how much harder it was going to make things for her.

Chapter Eleven

He stared at the ceiling, listening to the sound of the wind rustling through the trees outside, and wondered how the hell he was supposed to keep River off his mind.

They had spent the better part of the day together, and he couldn't stop thinking about her. No matter how much he tried to push her to the back of his mind, she was right there, insisting on taking up his brain space. If he was honest with himself, he didn't really mind.

She was just… There was something about her that drew him to her in a way he couldn't quite put into words. He liked her—liked the way she made him feel, how at ease and relaxed he felt when he was around her. And seeing her smile and interact with the people they'd seen in town had been a gift. He hadn't realized how much she'd needed that until he saw Mary fussing over her, and River's face lighting up as they talked about making clothes.

Now she slept just a few feet away from him, in the other room of the cabin. If she was sleeping at all. Maybe she was tossing and turning just like him. He hoped so. He didn't want these feelings he had to just go one way, but at the same time, he knew she had been through so much. He wasn't going to try and push her into something she wasn't ready for, even if he couldn't stop thinking about her.

It was getting late, and he knew he needed to get some sleep, but every time he closed his eyes, there she was, gazing back at him with that warm, open expression on her face. He couldn't help but wonder exactly what she had been through to bring her here, beyond the few details she had shared with him so far. He hoped that eventually she would share the rest of her story with him.

For now, he would just try to focus on figuring out his own life and not the growing attraction he felt between them. He had plenty of other things to think about—like his recovery and whether he was going to join Lawson's tactical operations team. Even though he knew his brother had some serious issues with it, Cade couldn't deny how much the idea appealed to him. It was a chance to secure a new direction in his life, and give himself something to focus on that wasn't the grueling reminder of everything he left behind.

He eventually drifted off to sleep and woke early the next day to the light peeking through the window next to him. He opened his eyes and lifted his head from the pillow, feeling a smile spread over his face before he could stop it. Something about waking up so close to River made him happy. Waking up in the same bed would be even better, but he quickly redirected his thoughts. He wasn't going down that road…not yet anyway.

He climbed out of bed before his mind could wander any further, and headed out to the small kitchen. He expected to see River there, but she must have already headed out to work. The door to her bedroom was open, and she was nowhere to be seen. He made himself a cup of coffee and sipped on it as he leaned up against the counter, watching as a few more leaves drifted down from the trees outside the cabin. He loved how peaceful it was this time of year.

He rinsed his mug and headed up to the lodge to grab some breakfast, and spotted River working on something in one of the rooms off the main corridor. Xavier must have gotten her set up with her own little space. He peered around the door to see her with a few needles pressed between her lips, brow furrowed as she fixed up one of the old windbreakers that looked as though it had seen better days. He thought about calling out to her, letting her know he was there, but thought better of it. He didn't want to throw her off her concentration.

He grabbed a quick breakfast and then headed to another physical therapy session with Carter. If he was lucky it would just be physical therapy today and no brotherly concern like yesterday.

"You know," Carter said casually while walking Cade through some mobility exercises. "Your physical recovery is just one aspect of a full recovery. You need to take care of your mental health too. You've been through a lot."

So much for no brotherly concern. "I know that," Cade said a little impatiently. "It's just easier for me to focus on the physical stuff right now." He'd never been great at talking about his feelings.

"You should go see our counselor here, Sarah," Carter told him, raising his eyebrows at his brother. "She could help you talk through the things that have happened and teach you some strategies for moving forward."

That sounded like torture to Cade. He'd rather run into

a burning building. "Why would I want to do that?" Cade asked.

Carter rolled his eyes skyward. "It's what this place is for, Cade. Helping people make a full recovery, which means both physically and mentally. You're nearly there when it comes to the physical side of things, but you have to focus on your mental recovery too."

"Yeah, okay, I'll think about it. Maybe I'll see if I can schedule her in," Cade replied to appease Carter.

Thankfully, Carter dropped it, and they spent the rest of the session talking about more neutral topics.

After he left Carter's office, he went to find Xavier to see if he needed Cade's help with anything. He enjoyed helping out around the lodge because it helped him stay busy and earn his keep. He also enjoyed it because it meant that he often ran into River throughout the day.

Like that very moment, as he saw her leaving the cafeteria. He couldn't help the grin that spread across his face.

He fell into step beside her. "Hey, how's your work going today?" he asked as they made their way from the cafeteria down to the room she had been working out of. She seemed happier today and she had a spring in her step that hadn't been there before. It was amazing what good rest and enough food could do for someone.

"Hi, Cade. I think I'm starting to make a dent," she replied with a grimace. "But there's still so much left that needs to be done. I think it'll take me the whole rest of the year to catch up with it."

Cade grinned at the thought. Having her around for at least another few months? It sounded good to him.

"I see Xavier moved you up from the basement. You like your new space?"

"Actually, I do. I've got a window so I can see outside and it's really helpful with the natural light coming in," she replied more animated than he'd seen her yet.

"That sounds nice. Well, keep up the great work and let me know if you ever need any help," he offered. "I'm not good with a needle but I am good company."

Her smile lit up her face. "I'll have to take you up on that sometime."

He really hoped she did.

THE NEXT AFTERNOON, when he was heading back to his cabin to grab a change of clothes after a gym session, he was waylaid by a woman he'd seen around but hadn't spoken to before. She stepped out in front of him, extending her hand and offering a smile.

"Hi. I'm Sarah Peterson," she introduced herself. "I'm the counselor here. Your brother mentioned that you might be interested in having a counseling session with me?"

Cade took her hand and silently cursed his brother for his meddling. He didn't want to seem rude, but he also didn't know if he was ready to talk about his feelings—especially with a stranger.

He shrugged noncommittally. "Yeah, he thought it might be good for me to have a couple of sessions to work through my…the stuff I've been through, I guess."

"I don't have any other sessions planned this afternoon," she remarked. "Are you free right now? We could cover the basics, lay down the groundwork for our future time together."

"Uh, well, I just left the gym and was going to change." He nodded in the direction of the cabins.

"Oh, I don't mind. People come to sessions from the gym all the time. But I can give you directions to my office and you can come down after, if you'd rather."

Cade really didn't want to do this, but if it would get Carter off his back, then so be it.

He nodded. "That sounds great. I'd really like to change, then I can come over," he replied.

Sarah quickly gave him directions to her office and he headed to his cabin with the promise he'd be there soon. He hurried to change and walked back to the lodge before he could second-guess himself, trying to give himself a pep talk on the way.

"Thanks for waiting," he said after knocking on the counselor's open door a short time later.

She smiled, pushing her glasses up her nose, and rose to meet him. She then gestured for him to take a seat while she closed the door. "Let's get started."

As she sat back at her desk, she offered him another warm smile. Cade couldn't relax, though. He didn't like talking about what had happened to him, what had led to his discharge from the military. He hated remembering and he did everything he could not to ponder on it any longer than he needed to.

"So," she began, clasping her hands together on top of her desk. "Let's start from the beginning. Can you tell me about your time in the service?"

He launched into his story—this part, he had no problem discussing with her, the part where everything had been going right. He had been sent to Afghanistan with his unit, and they had worked to free a city from the control of an oppressive terrorist group. It had taken months of hard work, but when they had finally managed to pull it off, he felt like he had found the career he needed. It was exciting and stimulating; he got to help people, and it kept his mind and body busy. It might not have been completely safe all of the time, but when was anything worth doing ever safe?

He had stayed out there for another couple of years, taking brief breaks to come back to America to see his brother. But he had been so focused on helping the people they had liberated, he didn't need anything else.

"And I think it would have stayed that way too," he remarked, with a sigh. "Until…until the ambush."

"The ambush?" she asked, scribbling on the page in front of her.

He nodded, and began to recount the story to her. He could still remember the day as clearly as if it were happening right in front of him. The heat from the midday sun beating down, the chatter in the truck as they transferred from one side of the city to the other. They had to take this little back road, nothing out of the ordinary—a lot of the streets had been damaged in the conflict, and it didn't give them room to move their trucks around with particular ease.

Then, he had heard it. The whistle of a projectile, swiftly followed by the sound of an explosion. One of their trucks had been taken out. Seconds later, chaos erupted.

He had thrown himself from the truck to try and help his comrades, but before he could, gunfire exploded around them, throwing up dust clouds in the sand. He had tried to use the truck for cover, but they were surrounded. A grenade was thrown close by, sending shrapnel flying into him. As he dove away from the blast, he'd caught a bullet in the shoulder.

"And that's the last thing I remember," he finished, shaking his head. "Next thing I knew, I was waking up in a field hospital, and they were telling me they were going to have to fly me back to the US."

She nodded, her face sympathetic. "That must have been so difficult for you, having to step away from the job that had become your identity at that point."

He grimaced. He hated thinking about it. Thinking about who he was before his injury and who he was now. He had purpose then, now he had no idea what his future looked like. He felt like he was floundering most days.

Cade sighed. "Yeah," he replied. "It's been hard."

And that was the most he would admit to. Even if it was the understatement of the century.

Chapter Twelve

Glancing around to make sure her bedroom door was firmly shut, River knelt beside her bed and pulled out the shoebox she'd found in the supply closet. Inside, she had been stashing any small supplies she'd managed to take from the main lodge. It wasn't much, but it was something—something she could focus on, something she could use to plan for the time when she had to move on, even if it made her feel guilty just thinking about it.

She tucked another spool of thread into the box, doing her best to push the guilt aside. She knew she couldn't stay forever; this was a temporary stop to rest and regroup before she moved on to find her family. She was really starting to settle in and enjoying her new day-to-day. It was going to be hard for her to leave when the time came.

Slipping the box back into place, she sighed and sat on the edge of her bed. It was strange to even think about leaving, after everything she had been through to bring her here. Living on the road had come so naturally to her before, but now that she had found this little corner of safety and security, leaving again seemed downright impossible. How was she supposed to just walk away from this place, especially when everyone had been so kind to her? At first she didn't give it much thought, assuming the others had ulterior motives for letting her stay. But the longer she'd been here, she realized differently. They were friendly and helpful to everyone; after all, that was what this place was about, helping and healing.

That was what she had to keep reminding herself. Not everything or everyone was out to harm her or cause her trouble. Just because she had been so used to it in her old life and always had to stay on guard didn't mean anyone here was looking to do the same thing. No matter how easy it would have been to believe it, she had to give them the benefit of the doubt until they gave her reason to think otherwise.

Hannah had been so sweet to her, and Xavier had given her a job. And Cade…well, Cade had been going around and around her head in a way she didn't know if she could deny any longer. Being near him, which she was a lot these days with them living together, made it feel like everything was going to be okay. Instead of the usual chaos in her mind, she felt like she could take a step back and relax.

She knew it was dangerous to let her guard down in any way, especially around him. There seemed to be some invisible force that pulled them together when they were around each other, especially alone. It would be a bad thing for her to get any more involved with him than she was already. He hardly knew anything about her but he seemed to care about her, even without all the specifics about her past and where she'd come from.

Maybe that would all change when he found out the truth, if she ever told him everything. All the more reason to keep it from him, she decided.

Outside her door, she heard Cade arrive, and she quickly checked to make sure the box was hidden out of view under her bed. Even though she had given him no reason to doubt her, she was always paranoid he would catch her doing something out of the normal and ask her questions she didn't want to answer. The last thing she needed was for him to figure out she was stealing supplies from the lodge and turn her in. They would definitely ask her to leave or, worse, notify the cops and have her taken away.

Taking a deep breath to settle her nerves, she stepped out of her room, and Cade raised his eyebrows when he saw her.

"I thought you were up at the lodge still," he remarked.

She shook her head. "Sorry, I'm here."

"No need to apologize," he replied, as he dropped his bag on the floor next to the couch.

"How was your day?" she asked, biting her lip as she watched him pull off his jacket. When he moved, the muscles beneath his shirt bulged slightly, and she felt a little tingle in her stomach.

"It was good," he replied, grinning. "I helped do a little gardening out near the edge of the forest. It's pretty out here this time of year. I also ran into Aaron, the handyman. We chatted a little and checked out the horses."

She returned his smile. "It really is nice. I heard the horses the other day when I was exploring a little. I actually meant to ask you or Hannah about them."

"We could walk over and see them sometime and maybe check out one of the trails while we're at it," he suggested.

"They do seem pretty quiet this time of year. I think I'd like them."

"Have you been hiking?" he asked. "Before you came out here, I mean?"

She shook her head. "Not as much as I'd like."

"So there's still plenty for you to explore," he agreed.

She nodded, her teeth resting on her bottom lip as she watched him. She couldn't help looking at his arms again. They were big, strong. The way they filled out his shirt, she wondered what they'd feel like wrapped around her.

She drew her gaze away from him, cursing herself for making it so obvious. She suddenly felt like a schoolgirl with a crush on a cute boy. She needed to get herself together. She couldn't just keep hanging around him like this, obsessing over every little moment they had together.

"I'm going to take a shower," she suddenly announced. She hurried into her room to grab her stuff, slipped into the bathroom and closed the door behind her.

She leaned back against the door and breathed deeply, trying to pull herself together. What was she doing? She needed to snap out of it. She couldn't let herself get attached to him. Even if he was the first guy to treat her kindly, maybe ever. She knew how much trouble she would be in if she allowed herself to get tied down, when what she needed was to keep her feet moving, keep herself heading toward her end goal.

Undressing, she flicked on the shower to let it warm up. The hot water could be seriously temperamental here, so she never took it for granted. She stepped underneath the rush of water, closing her eyes and tipping her head back, letting all her stress fade away.

See? She could do this. She was fine. She was still planning for what she was going to do next. A few weeks here to get her feet under her again, to get some decent food and rest. Save up some supplies. Then she could set out and look for her family once more. It might not have been easy, doing it like this, but it was easier than being out on the road with no idea where her next meal was coming from or—

"Ahhhhh!" she exclaimed, shrieking at the top of her lungs as the water suddenly turned from comfortably warm to freezing cold in an instant. She tried to jump back from the water, but bumped into the shower curtain behind her, bringing it crashing down around her.

"River?" Cade called out in a worried voice. She was too shocked and cold to speak. She grabbed the towel off the floor to try and warm herself up so she could tell him what had happened. But before she could answer him, the door flew open.

He looked panicked, his eyes darting around the bathroom and searching every corner before landing on her.

"Are you okay? What happened?" he demanded, catching her by the shoulders and looking into her eyes. "I heard you scream."

"I… I'm…" she began, but the sight of him like that made it hard for her to speak. He looked as though he was ready to fight whoever or whatever dared to cause her harm, ready to take on the unseen enemy on her behalf. She'd never in her life had someone step forward to defend her in such a way. She was stunned, grateful, excited…too many emotions to sort through in the short span of time. Now, as they stood opposite each other in that tiny bathroom, with Cade's strong hands gripping her arms, all she could do was stare at him. He was breathing hard, his eyes swirling with emotion as they bore into hers, and she suddenly found herself unable to resist.

Before she could stop herself, she leaned forward and kissed him.

His hands were still on her shoulders, but they dropped to her waist as soon as their lips touched, and he drew her in close. Their bodies pressed together, her arms went around his neck as his tongue slid into her mouth. The moment his tongue touched hers, they both moaned and Cade pulled her tighter into his embrace. It felt like time stopped and the only thing that mattered was the two of them, in that moment. Every worry, every doubt vanished instantly. She suddenly couldn't remember why it was such a bad idea to start something with him. She felt her heart slamming against her ribs, but this time, it wasn't fear that had caused it—no, it was want, desire, a need for him she had been doing her best to deny all this time.

The towel was the only thing between them, and she thought about tossing it aside. He groaned against her mouth as she tangled her fingers in his hair and pulled him impossibly closer. She sank deeper into him, their bodies pressed together from chest to hips and she still wanted to be closer. It was as though this was what they had both been waiting for since the moment they first laid eyes on one another.

And then, all at once, he pulled back. He was breathing hard, his lips slightly parted, his hands still gripping her waist and his eyes fixed on her, dark with desire.

He took a deep breath, closing his eyes and taking a step back. It felt like there was suddenly an ocean of space between them.

"I'm sorry." His voice sounded rough, and he forced his gaze from hers.

She furrowed her brow and shook her head. "No, Cade, I—"

"I shouldn't have come in here like that," he interrupted her, turning toward the door. "I'm sorry. I'll let you finish your shower in peace."

He quickly stepped out of the bathroom and pulled the door shut behind him, leaving her standing there wondering what had just happened. She reached up to skim her fingers across her mouth, trying to hold on to the memory of his lips on hers. She could still taste him, the sweetness of his kiss, his desire for her and hers for him. She now had a longing inside her, a craving she didn't know how to sate.

She sank down on the edge of the toilet and took a deep breath, trying to calm her racing heart. She had no idea what had just happened, but she got the feeling it was going to change everything between them, whether she wanted it to or not.

She looked around the tiny space, at the shower curtain that now lay in a heap in the tub and the rod askew against the wall, and sighed. She'd have to forgo the rest of her shower and ask Cade to reset the curtain.

First, she needed to get herself under control and dressed, then she'd address Cade and hope their kiss didn't make things more awkward than they already were.

Chapter Thirteen

Cade ran a hand through his hair as he stepped out of the cabin, trying to pull himself back together.

He couldn't think straight. The only thing he could think of was his lips on hers, the feeling of her body against his, nothing but a towel to keep them apart. How easy it would have been to just push that towel aside and…

No. He couldn't let his mind go there. No matter how tempting it might have been to finally give in to his desire, River had just left an abusive relationship and he did not need to complicate matters for her. The last thing she needed was for someone like him to come into her life, demand her attention when she was trying to find a safe place and heal.

When he had heard her scream in the shower, he hadn't even thought twice before going in there. How could he? He needed to know she was okay. After everything she'd been through, he couldn't help but wonder if it was all going to catch up with her, and he wanted to make sure he did everything he could to ensure she stayed safe.

But she deserved her privacy. She wasn't here because she chose to be for fun or just to pass time. She was here because she wanted to stop running, she wanted to feel safe and not have to look over her shoulder for her ex. And no matter how good that kiss had felt to him, he needed to remember that. Her being here was about what she needed, not him.

No matter how deep his attraction to River seemed to run.

He pulled his jacket over his shoulders and started back up to the lodge. He had been hoping to relax for the rest of the afternoon, but after their encounter, he knew he needed to give her plenty of space. He didn't want to make her uncomfortable or feel pressured into something she wasn't ready for.

The image of her wrapped in that towel and the kiss were both already burned into his brain. He knew he wasn't going to be able to forget either anytime soon, but he was going to have to do his best to shove his feelings aside so things weren't awkward between them. They still had to share a cabin, after all.

He wasn't going to push for more. If she wanted something from him, if she felt the same way for him that he did for her, then she would have to come to him. No matter how badly he wanted to turn right around and go back to their cabin and show her just what he had been imagining in those long nights he had spent alone in his bed.

He arrived up at the lodge just in time to see Xavier waving off the sheriff from the door. He frowned as he walked over to him.

"Hey, Xavier. What's that about?" he asked.

Xavier sighed, looking stressed. "There's been a break-in at one of the warehouses we get supplies from, about fifty miles from here," he explained. "The sheriff thinks it might have to do with that group he was telling us about before, the Shepards of Rebellion."

Cade nodded. "Yeah, I remember."

"I've told him we're going to have one of our teams look into it for him," he continued. "You think you could meet with Lawson and his team? Help with some tactical training? I don't think they're going to run into anything too heavy out there, but I'd rather they were prepared, you know?"

"Sure. Not a problem," Cade replied.

In truth, he was glad for the excuse to get away from his cabin for a while. He needed to clear his head, and he knew he wasn't going to be able to do that with River so close to him.

"What do you think's going on with these guys?" he asked, crossing his arms over his chest.

Xavier shook his head. "I have no idea, but this is the most worried I've seen Willis about any kind of trouble in the area," he remarked. "I don't know if he's just overreacting because all of this is new to him, or if there's actually something to it, but I'd rather be safe than sorry."

"Sure," Cade replied, frowning. He couldn't help but wonder if the Shepards drawing in closer to them had anything to do with River, but he quickly shook off that thought. He couldn't let his brain stray that way, not now. He had no idea what all she was running from, but he wasn't going to push her to come clean. Hopefully, when she was ready, she would trust him with her secrets.

The more time they spent together, though, the more Cade hoped she'd learn to trust him and tell him about her past. No matter how drawn to her he was or how much he wanted to pursue a relationship with her, they wouldn't be able to move forward until things were out in the open between them.

Just then, he saw Hannah approaching. Cade opened his mouth to greet her, but instead of stopping to talk, she narrowed her eyes in Xavier's direction and breezed right past them. He turned his head and watched her walk away at a fast clip.

Cade chuckled in surprise. "Damn, what's got her all angry?" he asked. "Did you do something to piss her off?"

Xavier shook his head as he watched her walk by, but Cade could tell there was more going on there than he wanted to admit to. He grinned. At least he wasn't the only one having woman trouble right now. It was totally unlike Hannah to be anything other than her bubbly self, so there was definitely something more going on under the surface than he knew.

This lodge had its fair share of secrets, more than Cade was sure he would ever know about. But right now, he couldn't worry about other people's secrets or problems.

He had enough of his own.

Chapter Fourteen

As River made her way back up to the lodge to continue her work for the day, she tried to push down the guilt stirring in her stomach.

How could she have kissed Cade like that? It was one thing to have a crush, but to actually do something about it? That was something else entirely. If he hadn't pulled back the way he had, she knew she would have wanted to go further. She would have gone all the way, and that would have tied her to him even more than she already felt now. No matter how much she wanted to be with him, she knew she could not allow that to happen. She had a plan and she needed to stick to it. Even if her heart wished things could be different.

She had to keep moving forward. She had to find Haven in New York and make sure her family was safe, make sure they had been able to leave behind the nightmare they had escaped for good.

And that wasn't going to happen if she found excuses to hang around the lodge and pretend like she didn't have a life outside of this place. Regardless of how tempting it might be, she had to get herself and her feelings under control. No more flirtation, no more making out, no more nothing.

She was going to throw herself into her work for the rest of the day and keep herself as busy as she could. Hopefully, Cade would be asleep by the time she got back to their cabin later and they wouldn't have to talk about what had happened between them. It was going to be over and done with, forgotten. Nothing more than a crazy mistake neither of them would mention again.

At least, she hoped so.

She arrived at the lodge and paused by the water fountain to fill up her bottle. A few people passed by her, but she didn't recognize any of them. She knew a few new guests had recently checked in to work on their recovery, but the new faces no longer bothered her like they did when she first arrived. She would catch herself hesitating slightly when several new people were around, but nothing like before, when she used to freeze in fear or hide until she was alone. She still found it best to stay out of the way, not to get distracted and focus on her work.

She dumped her bag on the floor to get her water bottle out, and it landed with a slight *bang*. Beside her, one of the men passing by froze on the spot, and then crumpled to the ground.

She recognized it at once, the way he reacted—the sound of her water bottle hitting the floor had brought a memory or experience to the surface so terrible that it caused him to physically react. She wasn't a doctor, but she'd seen PTSD before, and this looked like he was having a flashback.

He lifted his arms up to his head, clamping them around his ears as he balled up on the floor beside her. She felt horrible for causing his reaction. She glanced around, checking to see if anyone was coming to help him. When she didn't see anyone, she took a deep breath. Well, she wasn't going to leave him to deal with this alone. If she had to step in, so be it.

"Hey," she murmured, dropping down beside him. She knew that touching him could make it worse or cause him to unintentionally hurt himself or her, so she kept a small distance between them. The best she could do was to try to bring him back to the present instead of staying in whatever nightmare the sound of her bag clattering on the ground had caused him.

He didn't react to her, but she didn't get up. He needed to know that he was safe and that someone was here to help him, not hurt him.

"I don't know where you think you are right now," she continued, speaking slowly but firmly. "But the reality is that you're at the Warrior Peak Sanctuary, with me. My name is River and I work here. That sound you heard was my water bottle hitting the ground. I'm really sorry about that."

When he didn't react to her words, she decided to switch tactics. "You can feel the floor underneath you, right?"

He didn't reply for a moment, but he lifted his head. His eyes seemed glazed and distant, but he wasn't hiding from her anymore.

"Yeah, there you go," she continued. "You're here, right? Now, take a deep breath, feel the air go into your lungs. Now exhale. You're doing great."

He followed her guidance, and she talked him through his panic as best she could. Slowly, he began to unfurl from the ball he had pulled himself into. She coaxed him upright again, and she guided him to lean up against the wall as he breathed deep. She grabbed a paper cup and filled it with cold water and gave it to him to sip while he continued to calm down. Grabbing her bag, she was about to continue to fill up her bottle when she heard a voice behind her.

"Hey, there."

She turned to see a middle-aged woman with glasses standing behind her, smiling at her warmly.

"Hi," River muttered.

She was sure she was about to get told off for interfering with one of the guests. She had only been trying to help, but she really didn't have any idea what she was doing. She didn't want to cause any harm, but she couldn't leave that man on the floor in the middle of a crisis without at least trying to help. Especially since it was her fault.

The woman walked over next to the man, asking him a few questions to make sure he was okay. He assured her that he was doing better and she told him to come to her office later that afternoon so they could talk. When he nodded his agreement, she turned back to River.

"I'm Sarah," the woman introduced herself to River, extending her hand. "I'm the counselor here."

"River." She shook Sarah's outstretched hand. "I'm sorry about that, I didn't mean to… I mean, I was just trying to help him."

"No, no, you did a really good job," Sarah said. "You clearly knew what you were doing. Where did you train?"

River stared at her for a moment, shocked, and then shook her head.

"I, uh, I didn't train for anything," she muttered, feeling a little embarrassed to admit it. She was sure a woman like Sarah had probably gone through years of training, and here she was, standing in front of her, with hardly a clue of how to handle herself without looking like a total fool.

Sarah shook her head. "Wow," she replied in surprise. "You have incredible instincts, then. Have you ever thought about training as a therapist?"

"Uh, no," River answered. "I just... I've seen people act like that before and I just wanted to help. It was my fault after all. I dropped my bag and the noise startled him."

River tried to turn and walk away, but Sarah stopped her before she could get too far. River tensed up slightly, not sure exactly how this interaction was supposed to go, but deciding to see it through either way. She couldn't keep running from everything.

"You really did an amazing job with him," Sarah remarked, as the man turned in the opposite direction of them and continued on his way. "I've seen plenty of specially trained PTSD therapists who don't have the instincts you do, River."

"Thanks," River replied with a slight blush staining her cheeks. Was that a compliment? It felt like one. The way Sarah was smiling at her, it seemed like she was truly impressed with what River had done.

"If you're ever looking for something else to do around here," Sarah continued, "you come by my office, I could always use some help."

"Your office?" River replied, confused.

"Yes, to help out with some of my clients," she continued. "In a peer-mentoring type setting, since you don't have any formal training. But I think you could do a lot of good with people who are dealing with flashbacks."

River stared at her for a moment, trying to wrap her

head around the offer that was being laid out in front of her. There was a part of her that was flattered that someone like Sarah, who clearly knew what she was doing, would see potential in someone like her. But could she really risk creating any more connections to this place and the people here than she already had? The more ties she put down at the lodge, the harder it was going to be for her to leave when the time came.

River offered her a smile. "I'll think about it."

Sarah grinned back. "Wonderful," she replied. "Well, I hope I'll be seeing more of you, River. You did something really important with that man today. I hope you're proud of yourself."

River felt her face heat under the other woman's praise. She wasn't used to being complimented, and having a professional like Sarah tell her she had done something worthwhile made her chest warm in a way she hadn't felt in a long time. This place, it was full of people who seemed to see her differently than she saw herself. They saw more, even, than she knew she was capable of. They looked at her and didn't see a failure or a pathetic loser with no job skills to her name. They saw someone who was actually worth something.

As Sarah turned and walked away, River filled up her water bottle and pondered the offer. Maybe it would do her good, going outside of her comfort zone to help others who needed it. She didn't really know what she was doing, but it had felt good to help that man through his crisis. Heck, maybe she could even pick up some skills to navigate the pain she carried herself.

The offer was something she wanted to give serious consideration, but only if she stayed.

She could not think of making this detour on her journey permanent right now. She had other priorities to see to first—her family and all their safety. But maybe in the future, it would be something for her to consider. For now, she needed to remember her purpose for being here.

She arrived at the room off the lobby, where she'd been working. She appreciated Xavier letting her use this space instead of having to stay in the basement. River loved having a window to look outside. As soon as she stepped through the door, she felt her heart skip several beats in her chest.

Because she wasn't the only one there. No, someone else was in the room, inspecting her work like it was the most fascinating thing in the world.

It was Cade.

Chapter Fifteen

Cade wasn't entirely sure what he had hoped to achieve by coming to see her. He knew it wasn't a wise decision, especially after what happened earlier in the bathroom at their cabin. He should keep his distance, give them both a little space. He just couldn't seem to stay away, though. It was like an invisible force pulling him toward her.

River stopped on the spot when she saw him, and Cade grinned at her.

"Hey," he greeted. The tension in the air was thick between them, which didn't surprise him. How could it not be, after what had happened? Her lips slightly parted in surprise, and it took every bit of restraint he had not to lean forward and kiss her again, remind himself how good her mouth felt against his.

"Hey," she replied, her voice a little higher than usual.

She must have been able to feel the heat between them too. Even though he had stopped himself before things could go any further, he still wanted her so much it made his head spin.

"I was just checking to see if you'd made any progress on that winter jacket for me," he joked. He knew it was a lame excuse but it was all he could think of right then.

She smiled. "Not yet, but I haven't forgotten. I just need to find the right shade of pink for you."

"I trust you to know what looks good on me," he teased back.

She tucked a loose strand of her long hair back behind her ear. The way the light was coming through the window beside her, she looked almost radiant, as though she was exuding her own halo.

She flicked her gaze up to meet his, eyes darting back and forth as she looked at him.

Taking a deep breath, she spoke again. "Cade, I just… I wanted to apologize about what happened between us," she began, shaking her head. "I know I shouldn't have kissed you like that. It was just a spur-of-the-moment thing, and I know it's not appropriate, given that we're living together now."

"It's okay, River," he replied.

She shook her head. "No, no, it's not. And I need you to know it's not going to happen again. It was just…a mistake. You don't have to worry about me making it again."

"I'm not worried about it," Cade retorted quickly, trying to stop her before she went any further.

The last thing he wanted was for her to shut down any chance of that happening again, not when that kiss might have been the best damn kiss he'd ever had in his life. She didn't need to tell him she was sorry. He wanted to kiss her again, right then and there, wanted to pull her into his arms and—

But before he could say anything else, someone burst through the open door, and both of them turned to see what was going on.

"Cade," Xavier panted as he caught his breath in the doorway. "You need to grab your gear."

"What for?" Cade asked, furrowing his brow. This interruption really couldn't have come at a worse time. He didn't want to walk out of this room letting River think he didn't want to kiss her again, but the way Xavier had come barreling in there, it was clear something big was going on.

"Sheriff Willis called. We need to get down to the warehouse, *now*," Xavier told him. "The Feds are going to meet us there. We don't have time to waste. Come on, get moving!"

Cade shot a look at River, a silent apology for having to leave before they'd resolved what they were talking about. He really wanted to finish their conversation but Xavier was waiting and there was an urgency in his tone. He opened his mouth to find out more, but Xavier took off before Cade could ask him. River stepped forward, her eyes wide, her face colored with confusion.

"What's going on?" she asked, her voice shaking slightly.

Cade realized he couldn't walk out of there without calming her down at least a little, or she might assume this had something to do with her. That was the last thing he wanted.

"There's this group who've been causing trouble in the area for a while," he explained as quickly as he could. "They must be stirring up some problems again. The Feds just want us to help out, you know, with our training and all."

"What's the group called?" she asked. Her voice was taut, even as she tried to sound casual. He could tell she needed to know this before he walked away. Maybe it had something to do with what she had been running from.

"The Shepards of Rebellion," he answered, and at the sound of those words, all the color drained from her face. Her eyes widened, and she crossed her arms over her chest like she was trying to protect herself from something.

"Oh," she replied. He saw her trembling as she stood before him, pretending like she was okay. He took a step toward her, but she flinched back.

"River, are you okay?" he asked gently. "Do you...do you know who they are?"

She cleared her throat and tried to act casual. "Never heard of them," she replied, shaking her head.

He paused for a moment, searching her face. He wondered if he should push for more, but he could tell by the look on her face that she wasn't going to tell him anything else right now.

"We can talk later," he promised, and he turned to follow Xavier down the hall. He had run through a few basic protocols with the tactical team earlier, but he had no idea what he was going to be walking out into now. He wished they'd had more time to train as a team and be more prepared, but they would just have to figure it out as they went.

Despite that, he felt a nudge of excitement in his chest. It had been a long time since he'd been called into action of any kind, and though he didn't know if they were even going to be able to help out at all in this situation, he could feel the familiar adrenaline rush starting to pump through his body. He wanted to put all the skills into action that he hadn't been able to use since before his injury. The pain that sometimes throbbed in his shoulder seemed to have vanished, the pressure of it gone for now. Whatever this day threw at him, he knew he could take it.

He went back to the cabin to quickly change into some fatigues and strap on his weapons and gear, then he met up with Xavier at the front of the building. Lawson was nowhere to be seen, but Xavier had his arms crossed and he tapped his foot impatiently, clearly ready to get on the road.

"What do you know about what's happening?" Cade asked. His mind raced as he tried to figure out the best way to handle all this. The last thing he wanted was to make a mistake that might cost them, and it had been such a long time since he was out in the field, he was worried he was going to do just that.

"Not much," Xavier replied, checking his watch as though in a hurry. "We know the Feds are already down there, ready to move in. They're waiting for us as backup."

"They couldn't get anyone else out there?" Cade asked, frowning.

"They couldn't get anyone else down there in time. We're closer," he said, shaking his head. "You ready?"

"As I'll ever be," Cade responded. Cade and Xavier headed out to a truck parked just outside the main building. "Where's Lawson?"

Xavier narrowed his eyes. "He's already out there," he replied. "Didn't want to wait. We'll convene with him there."

"Right," Cade muttered, but in truth, he wasn't thinking about Lawson right now. No, he was thinking about River. He knew he should keep his mind on the mission but he couldn't stop thinking about the way she had reacted when he mentioned the name of the group they were going after.

What did she know about the Shepards of Rebellion? Had she encountered them in her time on the road? Maybe. They had been going after travelers, and she had been on her own long enough that she might have been a target if she wasn't being careful enough.

But the way she had responded, the way the blood had drained from her face, it seemed to Cade like it was more than that. As though the Shepards of Rebellion were tied to something she never wanted to think about again.

She would have just told him if they had mugged her or something, right? She had started opening up to him, a little at least. If something bad had happened, he thought she would have at least mentioned it to him.

But the fact she hadn't said anything about it made him wonder if something darker and more dangerous was going on. Something that might have been tied to the life she had tried to escape before. He could only imagine what she had been through and how bad it had been for her if she had been anywhere near those psychos. From what he'd heard about them, they got their claws into people and never let go.

What if she was one of them? It would explain why she had been so reluctant to talk about her past, if she had been wrapped up in something involving the Shepards.

Or maybe he was jumping to conclusions again.

Maybe he should just focus on what was right in front of him instead of trying to figure out what was going on with River. He had a job to do, and he needed to get his head in the game. He could worry about her and whatever she was keeping from him later. He'd be damned if he would be the cause of their team failing.

As Xavier pulled the truck away from the lodge, he couldn't help but glance back over his shoulder toward the building. That invisible string that drew him to River pulled hard. He wondered if she was watching them right now. Wondered if she was panicking as much as she seemed to be when he mentioned the Shepards.

But mostly, he wondered when she was finally going to tell him the truth about her past, and what had led her to be standing on the side of the road in the rain on that night he'd met her.

Chapter Sixteen

Her mind raced so fast she couldn't even stop to think straight. All she knew was that she had to get the hell out of there as soon as possible. She had to put as much distance between herself and this place as she could, and she needed to do it right now, before the Shepards caught up with her.

As soon as those words had come out of Cade's mouth, she knew there was only one thing for her to do—run. Immediately. No matter how much she wished she could stay, how much she wished she didn't have to do this, she didn't have a choice. If they were that close to her, even within fifty miles, she was in danger. And she was going to put everyone else in this place in the line of fire, too. She couldn't bear the thought of it. These people had been so nice and welcoming to her, she couldn't stand even the idea of causing them so much pain. They didn't deserve it.

But she knew Cade and the others would try to stop her if they were around when she ran, so she had to take the chance while they were away. She waited until after she saw Cade and Xavier drive away to make sure they were really gone then went back to the cabin to gather the supplies she'd managed to put together.

Even though the cold was really starting to set in, she

had to get on the road again. Fast. If she had learned one thing from these last few months, it was to trust her instincts, and they were screaming at her to get as far from here as fast as she could. The sooner, the better.

Her hands shook as she ripped open her bag and started stuffing it with all the supplies she had managed to secure so far. There wasn't much, but it was more than she had set out with the first time around. If she had made it this far before, she could do it again.

She was doing her best to convince herself, even though all she wanted was to curl up in a ball and hide. Her heart hammered in her chest, and she was sure she had given away the truth of at least some of her past to Cade when he had mentioned the Shepards to her. If he hadn't been so distracted by the mission he was going on, she had no doubt he would have taken the chance to interrogate her. And when he found out the whole truth, he wouldn't have wanted anything to do with her. How could he? He would want to put as much distance between the two of them as possible, and she wouldn't blame him.

She sealed up her bag, her hands shaking, and tried to steady her breathing. She wished there was a vehicle she could take, or even a bike. But they would notice the absence and someone would come after her before she got far enough way. Either one of them or the cops. That would be even worse. No, she was going to have to leave on foot, like before. She'd walk as long as she could before finding a place to hole up for a bit and make a new plan.

At least this time she'd have the rations she'd stocked and the clothes she got in town. She'd make a quick detour to the basement in the lodge and grab another sleeping bag, then be on her way. With winter coming in soon, she'd need the extra layers and protection.

She tried to take a deep breath as she swiped away tears that had started to fall from her eyes. It was going to be okay. It had to be. This had only been a stopping point, a short rest. She'd known she'd have to move on soon. That was why the thought of leaving had never been far from her mind. Yet, the thought of leaving the friends she'd made and Cade... His name alone sent a sharp pang through her chest.

She should have known better than to let her feelings get in the way, especially when it came to Cade. Whatever she felt for him, whatever they had stirring between them, it was nothing more than a pipe dream. A fantasy she had concocted based on a truth that was never real. He could never be with someone like her. He was so kind, so caring, so protective—because he thought she was on the run from an abusive ex, not that she had been part of a group like the Shepards of Rebellion. The very group he was out to help stop now.

Stepping out of her room and into the cabin's small living area, she noticed Cade's jacket draped over the back of the couch. He must have forgotten to take it with him when he left. She grabbed it without thinking and lifted it to her face, inhaling his woodsy scent. It would be the only thing of his she could take with her, the only reminder of him she would be able to cling to when she was out on her own again. She hoped he wouldn't mind her taking it. Maybe he would be able to forgive her if he knew what she was saving him from. How bad things would have been if she hadn't left while he was gone and he found out about her connection to the Shepards. The danger she could have brought to their door. It was better this way.

She put the jacket on, almost laughing at how it swallowed her small frame, and hooked her bag over her shoulder, readying herself for what was to come next. Throwing open the door, she sprinted out and ran straight into Hannah, who was hurrying down to her own cabin.

"Oof!" Hannah exclaimed as they crashed into each other. River stopped dead in her tracks, cursing to herself silently. She should have checked that no one was around. She had hoped she would be able to make a clean getaway, but now that Hannah had run into her, it was going to be next to impossible to make it out without drawing more attention to herself.

River looked up, and her heart twisted when she saw that Hannah's eyes were wet with tears.

Her eyes widened in horror. "I didn't hurt you, did I?" she gasped.

Hannah shook her head. "No, no, I'm fine," she replied, but River could tell that wasn't true. In the short time she'd known her, River had never seen her this upset, especially not in tears. She was always bubbly and had a smile for everyone. It was obvious to her that Hannah was definitely *not* fine right now.

"Hannah, what's going on?" she asked, already panicking that this had something to do with her. Hannah sniffed, and River put an arm around her and guided her down to her own cabin.

Once they were inside, River set about trying to make her some coffee. It took her a few minutes to figure out how to use the coffee machine, but eventually she pulled it off, and handed Hannah a steaming mug as she sat down opposite her.

"What's going on?" River asked again, concern dripping from her voice. She would never forgive herself if she had managed to bring some kind of danger to this place or if she had landed Hannah in trouble because of what she had been keeping from them all this time.

"I... I don't even know anymore," she admitted, shaking her head. There were dark rings underneath her eyes, and it looked as though she hadn't slept properly in days.

"You can tell me," River urged her. "It's okay."

Hannah sighed, lifted the coffee to her lips and took a long sip.

"I don't know where to start," she confessed. "It's all been going on for so long, I guess, I just got used to nothing ever happening between us, you know?"

"Happening between who?"

"Between Xavier and me," she replied.

River's eyes widened. "Wait, there's...there's something happening with you guys?"

"That's the problem, I don't even know," Hannah replied. "I... I've had feelings for him for a long time. Ever since I was a kid, pretty much. Him and my brother, Lawson, they've been friends for years—best friends. I knew he was always off-limits, so I never even thought about making a move. But the more time that passed, the harder it became to pretend I didn't feel the way I do about him."

River's eyebrows rose as she listened to Hannah. She had noticed some tension between Xavier and Hannah, but she had no idea this was where it came from. Not knowing either of them well, she'd assumed it was something work related, not personal.

"I know, I know," Hannah added, shaking her head when she saw the look on River's face. "It's such a mess. I don't know what it was, but I just… I decided I had to tell him the truth. So… I did. I told him how I felt."

"And?" River prompted.

"He kissed me," she replied, a smile brushing across her lips at the memory. "I told him I had been in love with him for years, and he…he kissed me. He didn't say anything back, but he didn't have to. I knew what was going on in his head. I knew…" She trailed off again, shaking her head.

"But someone saw, and they told my brother," she continued. "And he's furious. I mean, I always knew he would be upset. I knew he warned Xavier to stay away from me years ago, but I had no idea he would take the news this badly. He's so angry at both of us. Livid. I don't know what kind of damage it's done to their friendship, or our relationship, or…any of it, really. It's such a mess and it's my fault. I should never have said anything."

"You can't keep your mouth shut about something like that," River replied at once. "If the two of you have feelings for each other, you can't let your brother get in the way of that."

Hannah smiled a little sadly. "Yeah, I guess," she murmured, and then she seemed to notice what River was wearing for the first time. She stared at her for a moment, eyes sliding up and down her outfit, taking in the bag on her shoulder and Cade's jacket wrapped around her.

"Why are you dressed like that?" she wondered aloud. "You going somewhere?"

River hesitated before she responded. Could she tell her the truth? She would feel bad keeping her mouth shut when Hannah had just told her something so personal.

She could tell her a piece of the truth, at least. That was something, right? She slipped the bag from her shoulder and set it on the floor next to her.

"I… I was worried about Cade," she confessed. "I thought I would go after him and see if there was some way I could help."

"At this raid thing?" she asked with wide eyes.

River nodded. "Yeah, that's what I was thinking," she replied with a half-hearted laugh. "I know it's crazy."

"It's not crazy," Hannah assured her, smiling sweetly. "You…you have feelings for him, don't you?"

River bit her lip. If she said this next part out loud, there would be no more hiding from the truth, no more pretending like she didn't feel the way she did about this man. But maybe there was something to be said for being honest. Maybe it was time for her to confess how she felt, and share it with someone she knew she could trust. Hannah had just told her about her love life, after all. River might not have had much of one yet, but she needed to talk to someone about it.

"Yeah, I do," she replied. "I can't get him off my mind. I know it sounds crazy because we don't know each other that well yet, but I really like him."

"Hey, I can't blame you," Hannah replied, managing a laugh. "He's really hot. And the two of you have been living together. Has anything…you know…happened between you yet?"

"We kissed," River admitted.

Hannah clapped a hand over her mouth. "Oh my gosh, really? That's so great," she gushed, and River couldn't help but smile. It felt good to finally talk to someone else about it, to admit her feelings out loud. It felt like a tiny weight had been lifted. Hannah might not have known the whole story, but it had been a long time since she'd had a girlfriend she could talk to about stuff like this.

"Yeah, and I think I'm really falling for him," she continued. "I don't know what's happening between us, and I don't want to push him. I know I should have more self-control around him."

"Girl, have you seen the way he looks at you?" she exclaimed. "He's the one who's been needing the self-control out of the two of you."

"You really think so?" River asked, chewing her lip. It had been so many years since she'd had anything resembling a normal relationship, she could hardly remember what it felt like to have someone show interest in her. How was she supposed to recognize it? But if Hannah seemed to think there was something going on there, maybe she wasn't imagining his attraction to her.

"Yeah, I really do," Hannah replied, reaching over to give her hand a squeeze. "And you deserve it, River. After everything you've been through, you deserve someone like Cade."

River wasn't sure if she entirely believed that yet. But she knew, at least for the time being, that she wasn't going to be able to leave now. She couldn't go back to living on the road, on the run. So maybe she should get used to sticking around here for a little while longer.

Even if the thought of remaining in this place with the Shepards potentially so close by scared the hell out of her.

Chapter Seventeen

As the truck pulled to a stop outside the warehouse, Cade opened the door and jumped out. The adrenaline was pumping and it had taken all the restraint he had not to leap out of this truck half a mile down the road and sprint the rest of the way there.

It was a cold day, clear and bright, and Lawson stepped out of the doorway to the warehouse and waved them over. An FBI agent stood next to him. Cade recognized the regulation haircut and the windbreaker those types always wore.

"Hey," Cade greeted Lawson, as he joined them. "What's happened? What did we miss?"

"They're long gone now." Lawson sighed. "But they did some real damage to this place. And the owner? He was unlucky enough to be here when they arrived, and they beat the hell out of him. Put him in the hospital. He's recovering now, but his jaw's wired shut, so there's not much he can tell us."

"And they think it was the Shepards?"

"They know it was," he replied, shaking his head as Xavier caught up with them. "There were reports from people who saw them passing through a small town not far from here. But law enforcement couldn't intercept them in time to stop this."

"And they raided this place for supplies?" Xavier asked.

Lawson shot him a look, then turned his attention back to Cade, addressing him and not Xavier.

"Looks like it," he said. "Best we can do now is take a look around the place and get an idea of what they took. This place is usually a storage facility for survivalist supplies—canned food, stuff like that—but they have a decent amount of weaponry too, most of it smaller handguns and a variety of ammunitions. If they've taken off with a lot of that, they could be planning an attack somewhere."

"We'll take a look," Xavier volunteered.

Lawson didn't even look at him before he headed over to the truck to fill the other guys in on what had been happening.

"What is going on between the two of you?" Cade asked, as Xavier watched Lawson walk away.

Xavier shook his head. "You don't want to know," he replied. "It won't get in the way of what we're here to do. Come on, let's see what we've got."

Cade raised his eyebrows, but knew better than to push for more information, especially in the middle of a mission. They had a job to do here, and what mattered was getting it done, not figuring out whatever drama was going down between them.

They headed into the warehouse, and Cade grabbed an inventory paper from where it had been dropped next to the front door. He scanned the space—it was all in disarray, and it looked as though they had taken almost everything they could get their hands on.

"Do you think they were looking for something specific?" Cade asked Xavier as they started to make their way in and out of the rows of tall shelving that had been knocked over to figure out what had gone missing.

"I honestly don't know," Xavier replied. "I'm still trying to figure out what they're doing this far north."

"Oh, yeah?"

"Yeah, I've been doing some research into them since Willis said that the Shepards might become our problem soon," he explained. "And they've never really come this far out of their territory before. I can't figure out what it's about, but there has to be a reason."

"You don't think they're just trying to expand their territory?" Cade asked.

He shook his head. "The movements they've been making, it's more than that," he replied. "There's something he's looking for out here. I'm not sure what it is. Hell, I'm not sure if he even knows what it is, but there's a reason behind it, I'm sure of it. They might be crazy, but they don't do things for no reason."

"He?" Cade locked on that one word. "You talking about the guy who runs the Shepards of Rebellion?"

"Ryker," Xavier stated. "That's his name. There's not a whole lot out there about him, but what I do know is that he's some seriously bad news."

"In what way?" Cade inquired. The more he knew about this guy, the better. If there was one thing he had learned during his time in the Special Forces, it was to learn as much about your enemy as you could.

"The way he treats his followers," he replied. "There aren't many who have managed to get away, but those who have all say the same thing. That he uses them like possessions. He doesn't let anyone else get close to them, totally cuts them off from their friends and family. Shuts off their connections to the outside world so they don't have anything other than him. It's crazy. He really is running a cult out there."

Cade nodded as he thought about what Xavier had said. He'd known men like that before. Men who treated everyone else like they were owed something. They were some of the most dangerous out there, some of the most ruthless. Whatever this Ryker guy was looking for out here, he wasn't going to stop until he got his hands on it, or until someone got in his way and couldn't be pushed around like everyone else.

"You think the Feds will get him?" Cade asked as they started to take the inventory.

Xavier shrugged. "I don't think they're confident about it, and I can't say I blame them. He's been running this gang for years now, and nobody has managed to get close enough to bring them down. But leaving his territory like this, he might open himself up to the possibility of being caught. He's not going to be as strong out of his usual hunting ground in Florida."

"Right," Cade muttered. There was something about even hearing of this Ryker guy that made the hair on the back of his neck stand on end. He was obviously really bad news. And even though Cade was used to handling trouble during his time in the military, he didn't like not knowing what they were dealing with when it came to this guy and the gang he ran.

"Let's start at the back and work our way forward," he suggested to Xavier.

Lawson still hadn't come in to join them. There was clearly something serious going on between the two men, but it was the last thing on Cade's mind right now. They had intel to gather, and the more they could find out, the easier it was going to be to track this Riker guy down and stop his gang before they moved any farther across the country.

Cade handed Xavier the inventory sheet and headed to the back of the warehouse, where some of the shelving was still upright.

"Okay, so bottom shelf is…" he began, but before he could get any further, a man sprang out from behind the shelves.

"What the hell?" Xavier exclaimed.

Cade managed to step to the side before the man could make contact with him.

The man, who appeared to be in his midforties, looked panicked as he followed Cade's movement. Cade saw his chest rising and falling and his eyes darting around as he tried to find a way out. The man took a swing at him, but Cade dodged it easily. His hand flew into the metal shelf behind Cade instead. The clanging noise filled the warehouse, and the man let out a cry of pain, drawing his hand back in shock. Cade moved toward him to try and capture him, but the man surprised him, slamming his forehead into Cade's jaw and sending him reeling back. Cade clutched at his face, the pain not registering yet as he tried to figure out how best to handle this.

"Xavier, cut him off," Cade called to his friend, gesturing to the other end of the row before the man could turn that direction to run. Cade might not have known exactly what this man was doing here, but he was sure they could get something useful out of him.

The man tried to beat Xavier to the other side, but Xavier managed to catch him before he could get away. He almost squirmed loose of Xavier's grip, but Cade grabbed him before he could continue his escape, and pinned him to the ground with his hands behind his back.

"Xavier, get the others so we can make sure there's no one else hiding in this place," Cade said, still holding the man to the ground. His arm twinged with pain, but he hardly felt it. He hadn't expected an attack here, but his instincts had kicked in without a second thought. It felt good to be back in action.

Moments later, the warehouse filled with noise as the rest of the guys came flooding in. The man had given up trying to escape from Cade's grip, as though he knew there was no chance for him now.

Who was he? Had the Shepards left behind one of their own, or was this someone else entirely? He didn't have a clue.

But they had someone here, at least. Someone they could use to shake out a little more information about this gang.

And that was more than they'd had before.

Chapter Eighteen

She paced back and forth in the cabin as she waited for Cade to return, wondering how much longer they were going to be away from the lodge.

It had been nearly a day since she had last seen him, and her mind had been torturing her with questions about where he was and what was happening to him. She didn't know if she could take much more of the waiting.

She was so worried about him, worried about what might have happened out there. What if he had encountered the Shepards? She knew all too well what they were capable of. If he had been hurt as a result of going after them, she would never be able to forgive herself. Because she knew what they were doing here, and that it was her fault they had managed to creep their way across the states and so close to the lodge.

This place should have been safe. It was what they had tried to create here, a space where those dealing with physical or mental trauma could recover. The thought of being the one to ruin that was more than she could take.

And after the talk she'd had with Hannah, River had decided she needed to tell Cade how she felt about him. She couldn't leave this place with it unsaid. Even if it might be more complicated than she was able to wrap her head around, he deserved to know. She needed him to understand that her feelings for him were real. That even though she had not been completely truthful and open about her past, when she looked to her future, she wanted him to be a part of it.

She had fallen asleep on the couch waiting for him to come back to their cabin, and now it was the next morning and there was still no sign of him—no sign of anyone who had gone out on that mission, actually. She had the brief thought about going out to try to find him, or even asking Hannah if she knew where they went and ask her to take River there. She knew that was crazy, though. She needed to keep her head on straight and her emotions under control and wait for him to return.

Finally, she heard it—the sound of an engine, the rumble of a truck heading up the path to the lodge. They were back? They were back! She threw open the door and hurried out toward the lodge, sprinting to catch up with them by the time they reached the entrance. She prayed Cade would be with them.

Sure enough, the truck drew to a halt outside the lodge, and Cade was one of the first ones out. She rushed toward him, but as she got closer she began to slow down. There was a large bruise forming over his jaw. What had happened to him?

"Cade!" she called to him, and he turned toward her voice. When he saw her, a smile spread over his face, followed by a wince as he stretched the painful-looking bruise on his jaw.

"Are you okay?" River demanded, grabbing his hand

and squeezing tight. She was just so glad he was there right now, she couldn't think of anything else, even to ask what had taken them so long or how the mission had gone.

But before he could respond, others who had been with him came pouring out of the truck, splitting Cade and River apart once more. Cade locked eyes with her, giving her a nod as though to let her know that everything was okay, but she could tell it wasn't. This was the most action she had seen at the lodge since she had arrived here, and she was worried that it had to do with her. Concerned that she might have brought more danger to their door and left them all unaware by not being up-front when she arrived.

Some of the men hurried back in to the main lodge, talking over each other while a few still hung around outside. There was an excited buzz in the air, which she took as a good sign, but she was still confused as to what had actually happened. Why wasn't anyone attending to Cade? They must have had something more important to focus on right now.

Finally, everyone vanished inside and she and Cade were alone again. She rushed over to Cade and stared up at him, her brows tight with worry.

"Are you okay?" she asked again.

He nodded and smiled down at her. "I'm okay."

"What happened to your face?" she asked, reaching up to touch the bruise on his jaw without thinking. He winced and pulled back.

"I'm sorry, I'm sorry," she blurted out. "Did someone hurt you?"

"I got attacked when we were at the warehouse," he explained, and her stomach clenched with panic.

"Attacked?" she whispered.

"It's okay, though," he replied. "He didn't manage to do much to me. We got him under control."

He? Her mind began to race as she tried to figure out who it might be. Surely it couldn't be Ryker, right? They wouldn't have been able to subdue him so easily. He would need a whole army to take him down. That man was evil. And he probably wouldn't have let Cade walk away with nothing more than a bruise on his face.

"This is my fault," she muttered under her breath, she was sure of it.

"What are you talking about?" he replied with a frown, cupping her face in his hand.

She shook her head and drew her gaze away from him. She didn't want to tell him, but the truth was she had dragged them into this. If she hadn't arrived here, he would never have gotten hurt.

And if she stayed, he was only going to get hurt again, and again, and other people would too. Other people who had come here for safety only to be met with the danger that would follow her wherever she went. Guilt stabbed at her hard. She needed to go. She should have left the night before when she'd had the chance. But after she had spoken to Hannah, she had made herself believe for a moment that she could find a way to make it all work.

But looking at Cade now, she knew she couldn't. Tears brimmed in her eyes and dripped down her cheek, and Cade wiped them away with his thumb. She squeezed her eyes shut and tilted her head into the palm of his hand, wishing she could stay here, in this moment. She wished she could tell him everything and promise that it would all be okay, even though she knew it wasn't the truth. How could anything ever be okay again after what had happened? She knew what the Shepards were capable of, and it was only going to get worse from here. She didn't want to put more of a target on the lodge or the people living here than she already had.

Before her mind could stray any further back down that path, she heard voices behind her. One voice she recognized. A voice that made her feel as though she was about to throw up on the spot. She spun around, trying to place it.

All at once, she figured it out. Cade turned back to the truck and helped Lawson and Xavier guide out someone she had never seen at the lodge before.

But he wasn't a stranger to her. He lifted his gaze up from the ground as though he could sense her presence, and his face drained of color when he saw her. He froze on the spot, not taking his eyes off her. Staring at her like he had seen a ghost.

"River?" he breathed.

Hearing the man say her name made her knees tremble, the panic starting to set in. After all this time, after as far as she had managed to get from them. Right here in front of her was a remnant of her old life—a part of her past she had prayed she would be able to get away from for good.

"River, what are you doing here?" he demanded.

Chapter Nineteen

Cade looked from the man to River and back again. River looked as though she was about to be sick right there, hardly able to draw in a breath, and the man stood frozen, like he had seen someone he had never expected to lay eyes on again.

"Wait, do you two know each other?" Xavier asked with a frown.

River shook her head and looked at the ground, but the man nodded.

"River, don't you remember me? It's Louis. Dr. Louis."

She wouldn't even look at him. Wouldn't look at any of them. Cade put an arm around her waist and she leaned into him like he was the only thing keeping her upright in that moment. He squeezed her in close, and felt her body trembling helplessly against him as she tried to pull herself together.

"I want the two of them in my office, *now*," Lawson demanded, snapping his fingers and making her flinch. "River and Dr. Louis both have some explaining to do."

River tried to pull away from Cade, but he kept a firm grip on her. She needed to face this, whatever it was, but he wasn't going to let her do it alone. No matter how she knew this guy, no matter what had happened between them in the past, she had to come clean and tell them what she knew. This man had been found at the location of a break-in by the Shepards, after all. Did that mean she knew something about them, too?

Cade guided River into the lodge, where Xavier and Lawson steered the man—the doctor—to Lawson's office. Cade's mind reeled as he took it all in. Maybe it was the hit he'd taken from the doctor still scrambling his head, but he couldn't make sense of it.

Xavier and Lawson went to get coffee before they began their interrogation, leaving Cade, River and the man who called himself Dr. Louis waiting in the office. Louis stared at River but she wouldn't look him in the eyes. Instead, her eyes darted nervously around the room.

"River, you must remember me," he said in a soft voice.

She stood stock-still, eyes pinned to the wall next to him. A tear ran down her cheek, but she hardly seemed to notice it was there.

"You're looking for Haven, aren't you?" he asked her.

She still didn't respond, but she began to shake when he said that name. Who was Haven? Cade was utterly lost as he tried to figure out how River knew this guy. He knew they were going to get to the bottom of it one way or another when the others got back.

Lawson and Xavier returned, taking their seats behind the desk and gesturing for the rest of them to do the same. Although Louis had fought them when they'd first met, he'd been surprisingly cooperative when they'd told him they were working with the Feds. He had allowed himself to be transported up to the lodge without too much more of a fight, even apologizing to Cade for headbutting him.

"So," Lawson began, raising his eyebrows at the doctor. "Are you going to tell us who you are?"

"I'm Louis," the man replied at once, shooting another look at River like he was trying to figure out if she was going to say anything. "I... I'm a doctor. Or, at least, I was. I've been working as an informant for the last few years against the Shepards of Rebellion."

Xavier narrowed his eyes. "How do we know you're working against them and not with them?" he asked, leaning forward.

"I can't prove it to you, but trust me, I wouldn't have come so quietly if I was a bona fide member," he replied. "I've been acting as their doctor for a long time now, but I've been feeding information to the Feds the whole time."

"Can we confirm that with our contact?" Lawson asked, and Xavier nodded, getting to his feet to take care of the request. Once he was out of the room, the doctor continued.

"I'd heard them mentioning you before, the Feds I was working with," he explained. "Ever since the Shepards started moving on a little farther north, things have been... changing. It's been harder to stay on top of everything that's going on. But when I saw what they'd done to that man, the one who owns the warehouse, I... I just couldn't continue. I couldn't keep standing by and pretending anymore. That's why I broke with them. I didn't feel as though I had a choice."

His voice hitched in the back of his throat as he spoke, and Cade wondered just how much he had seen over the years he had been an informant for the Feds on the Shepards of Rebellion. How much had he had to keep his mouth shut about?

And how did River tie into all this? That was the part he couldn't make sense of. Was it like he had suspected, and she was part of the Shepards? Was that who she had been on the run from? Was someone in that group the ex she had fled from, or had that just been a cover story?

Xavier returned to the office and nodded at Lawson.

"He's telling the truth," he replied. "He's been working with the Feds for the last few years on this."

"If there's anything you need to know or anything I can help with, please just let me know," the doctor told them, glancing between Xavier and Lawson. "I know you're helping with the case, and trust me when I say you're going to need every advantage you can to bring these guys down. I've seen what they can do, how far they'll go…"

He trailed off. A shiver seemed to run through the room. The enormity of what they were facing wasn't lost on Cade. This man had been ready to fight his way out of the situation he'd found himself in to get away from the gang. Cade could only imagine how bad things had gotten for him. How terrified he must have been that he was going to be exposed at any given moment, and what it might have meant if he had been.

River still stared at the wall, tears falling silently down her cheeks. It was clear being close to this guy had triggered something in her, drawn a memory back to the surface she didn't want to even think about.

Finally, the doctor turned his attention to her again. He dropped his voice slightly, leaning toward her. She recoiled from him at once, like he was toxic.

"They don't know where you are, River," he assured her, his voice gentle. There was clearly a history between the two of them, even if it was a history she wanted to forget.

His mind flashed back to when he had first met her, how fearful and jumpy she had seemed. Was it because she knew she was being chased? Because she knew she couldn't leave behind her old life as easily as she wanted to?

"You're probably in the safest place you can be," he continued, and River let out a sob.

Cade had seen her cycle through plenty of emotions in the time that he'd known her. But this? This was unlike anything he had seen before, and he would have been lying if he said it didn't worry him to see her like this. He wanted to pull her into his arms and tell her it was all going to be okay, but he knew she wouldn't have believed him. Whatever she had been running from, it had well and truly caught up with her now, and there was no way she could pretend otherwise. Whatever she had been heading toward, whoever Haven was, she had halted in her search for her, staying at the lodge and trusting them instead of moving forward.

Trusting him to protect her against her past.

Lawson and Xavier flicked their gazes between the doctor and River. Lawson's face bristled with anger, an anger Cade could only guess came from knowing how much trouble River had brought right to their door. Despite that, though, Cade felt protective of her. He would do anything to make sure that whatever nightmare was following her didn't get any closer than it already had.

The doctor reached for River's shoulder, but she pulled

back from him, letting out a whimper. Xavier eyed the two of them skeptically, trying to piece together what was going on. Cade wasn't even sure what was actually going down, but he stayed by River's side, not wanting to break away from her for a second. She seemed to have been doing so much better in these last few days, so to see her so upset and scared like this made him feel…angry. Angry, knowing there were people out there who had given her reason to feel this way. People who had scared her and hurt her enough in the past to turn her into this terrified woman before them now.

"Take our new friend to get some lodging," Lawson told Xavier. "Make sure there are guards on the door at all times."

"I'm not going to try and go anywhere," Louis replied.

Lawson shook his head. "It's not about you getting out," he replied grimly. "It's about others getting in."

Cade nodded in agreement. He couldn't imagine that the Shepards wouldn't notice one of their own had gone missing, and when they did, they might put the pieces together about what he had been doing while he'd been with them. They didn't strike Cade as the type to forgive and forget. Better to keep the doctor safe and get all the information out of him they could, than risk a break-in that would get him hurt—or worse.

Once Xavier had escorted the doctor from the room, Lawson turned his attention to River. His mouth was set in a hard line, his expression unreadable.

"River," he began, his voice low. He was doing his best to control it, not to spook her, but as soon as she heard her name, her whole body tensed.

"I think I need to talk to you. Alone."

Her eyes darted over to the door, and she didn't say a word.

Lawson's eyebrows shot up. "Don't you dare make a run for it—"

But before he could stop her, she dashed out the door and into the corridor beyond.

Lawson sprang to his feet. "Dammit," he muttered, and he went to follow her. But before he could, Cade put out his arm to stop him.

"Leave her," he told him firmly.

Lawson glared at him. "I need her to explain to me exactly what the hell she's doing here. And what her connection is to the Shepards."

"I know," Cade assured him. "You deserve an explanation. I get it. But don't go after her. She's terrified. She's not going to leave, I know that. Let me talk to her, okay?"

Lawson didn't exactly look happy about the suggestion, but he rolled his eyes skyward and let out a sigh. "Fine," he grunted.

Though his anger was evident, he was smart enough to see that Cade was going to get a whole lot more out of River than he would ever be able to. Cade nodded his thanks.

"I'll find out everything we need to know," he promised.

Lawson shook his head. "I hope so," he replied. "And I hope that woman you brought to our door isn't more trouble than she's worth."

Cade turned to leave the office, Lawson's words ringing in his ears. There was no doubt River had brought a whole lot of trouble with her—trouble beyond what Cade could ever have imagined when he had seen her by the side of the road, in that dirty homemade dress, looking like she had been living in the wild.

But no matter what kind of trouble she had chasing her, Cade knew one thing for sure: she was worth it.

Every bit.

Now he just needed to prove that to her.

Chapter Twenty

River felt the tears streaking down her face as she ran back to the cabin, but she let them fall unchecked. It felt as though she had gone back in time to relive everything again the moment she had laid eyes on Louis—the moment she had been reminded of a past she wanted nothing more than to leave behind. Her heart pounded in her chest, her body screaming at her to do one thing—run.

She should not have put off leaving as long as she had. She should not have let running into Hannah stop her yesterday. And now, with them at least suspecting her connection to the Shepards, thanks to Louis and her reaction to him, she was truly left with no choice. It was too dangerous here. Maybe she'd get enough of a head start that Ryker and the others wouldn't find her and they'd leave this place alone. And then there was Cade. Her heart clenched at the thought of him. He already knew more than she wanted him to and would probably be glad to see her go.

She arrived back at the cabin and started restuffing everything back into her bag that she'd removed the night before. This time, she wasn't going to be stopped, she wasn't going to let her emotions get the better of her. No matter how tempting it might be to stick around just a little while longer, she was leaving.

She would figure out which direction to go once she got back on the road. Eventually, she'd forget about her time here and her new friends she was leaving behind. They were definitely better off without her around to cause them unnecessary pain and bring danger to their door. She had no clue what the Shepards would do if they found this place, though she could guess from past experience. She didn't want these people to suffer any ill will trying to help her.

But before she could race out the door, Cade arrived at the cabin. She could barely even look at him. She tried to brush past him but he blocked off her exit, stopping her from fleeing.

"Hey, River, I need you to talk to me," he told her. "Lawson is practically blowing his lid back there. If you're going to stay, you need to tell us what's been—"

"I'm not going to stay," she shot back before he could get out another word. No point in pretending any longer.

"What are you talking about?" he replied, catching her arm before she could make a break for the door again. "Of course you are. You're not going anywhere. They're out there, you can't risk—"

"You don't understand, Cade!" she exclaimed, staring up at him, her eyes desperate. "They're coming after me. If I stay here, they're going to come to this place, and they're going to ruin everything you guys have worked so hard to build. I don't want that for you. I can't stand the thought of it. So will you just…just let me go? Please?"

His eyes were wide as he looked down at her, trying to take in what she had just said.

He shook his head slowly and crossed his arms in defiance. "If you think I'm going to let you walk out that door without explaining what you mean," he replied, "you've got another think coming, River."

Cade wasn't moving out of her way and River wasn't sure what to do next. She took a deep breath, trying to collect her scattered thoughts. She had to think of something to say to make him let her go. Every minute she stood there was costing her time and distance on the road. Bringing danger closer to them all.

But looking at Cade, seeing his confusion and the different emotions crossing his face…she couldn't just leave like this. He had given her so much in these last few weeks, a safety and security she didn't even know was possible for her. And a kindness she had been craving for longer than she could remember. The least she could do in return was tell him some part of the truth. She owed him that much.

"Fine," she muttered. "I'll tell you everything."

She sank down on the couch and dropped her bag at her feet. Maybe it was better this way. She was so tired of running, of being afraid of everything. She pulled her knees up to her chest and wrapped her arms around them like a shield. Her heart skipped a beat when Cade sat down beside her and wrapped one of her hands in his. The warmth of his touch was all she needed to get the words out. Hesitantly, she told him the story of what had brought her out here.

When she and her sister, Haven, were kids, their father had wanted to make a better life for them, the way so many fathers did, and so he'd started working for a shady character called Hector Neimons in the small town they lived in. Before long, Hector had brought him and his family into the Shepards of Rebellion, a biker gang that basically functioned as a cult worshipping at the altar of the Neimons family, especially Hector's son, Ryker. Even when things started getting darker and more dangerous, their hold on River's father was too intense.

River had grown up in a world of paranoia and violence, where every wrong move had been punished harshly. There wasn't a single choice she could make that wasn't scrutinized by the other members of the growing Shepards group. They were cut off from the rest of the world, only allowed to rely on the Neimonses for food and supplies. It was why she had learned to sew, so she could at least mend the tattered old clothes that they had given her to live in for years on end.

And she had been used to it. It had been normal for her, because she had never known anything else. Even when the crime and violence started getting out of control, she reminded herself of how much the group had done for her and her family, how they had supported them when they had been struggling.

Of course, she had to put to the back of her mind the fact that the gang had been the one to cause most of that struggle in the first place. Like when her father had been kept away from work for months because they were suspicious of his intentions. But it was easy to forget that part when everything she'd had—clothes, food, shelter—all came from them.

Eventually, it had become too much for her father, and he had decided he wanted to get his family out of there. It was when River was a teenager, and the thought of something new was tantalizing to her. She had to find out what there was in the rest of the world, what existed beyond the bounds of the life the Neimons family had created for her.

And so, her father started to put together a plan. It wasn't much at first, but it was something. They put away supplies, enough to cover them while they were on the road for a few weeks to find somewhere new. He seemed sure the gang would come looking for them, but he assured his family it wouldn't go much deeper than that. He swore they didn't care enough about the family for them to really try too hard to get them back. As long as River and her family kept their mouths shut about the gang and their criminal activity, they would be able to escape unharmed.

And maybe River had believed that at some point. Maybe she had trusted her father and actually allowed herself to believe that they would be able to get out, make a clean break and never look back. How naive she had been. But now, all this time later, she could see it had been nothing more than a pipe dream, a fantasy they had all been clinging to because the alternative was more than they could bear.

The alternative being that they were trapped, and there was no way out, no matter what they did.

That was how it went. On the night they were due to leave, they had everything packed up and ready to go. Haven and their mother were in the car, and River and her father were packing up the last of their stuff before they hit the road.

Before returning to the house to grab the last of their belongings, her father had given specific instructions to her mother for her to keep watch and if anyone approached, or there were any signs of trouble, then she and Haven should leave immediately. He'd get River and himself out and they'd rendezvous at a location her parents had already agreed upon.

But before they could get anywhere, a shot rang out.

"River, get down!" her father yelled to her, and she ducked back inside their small house for cover. Outside, she heard the roar of the engine and watched as her mother drove off with her sister. As soon as the dust had cleared, she saw her father's body sprawled on the driveway.

She ran to him at once, but it was too late. They had killed him. She cried out, suddenly all alone in the world. Her mother and sister had followed the plan and fled, and she was still trapped here, without even her father to rely on.

"Don't worry, River," Ryker had told her. "We'll take good care of you."

It sounded more like a threat than a promise.

And so, she'd stayed. She had nowhere else to go, nobody else to turn to. She just had to trust in herself, and pray that one day, she found a way out.

The Neimons family took good care of her. She was moved into their home so they could keep a better eye on her there, and she hated every moment of it. Someone was always watching her. Things only grew more and more dangerous as time passed. What had started out as little more than a ragtag group behind their leader soon began to build into something with real focus, something really violent and obsessive.

Even more so when Hector died and left Ryker in charge. Ryker was so much worse than his father. More of a control freak than Hector had ever been, and when it came to recruiting new members, he didn't wait for them to come to him. If he saw someone he liked the look of, he would snatch them up and brainwash them until they didn't have any choice but to go along with the sick, twisted nightmare he dragged them into.

River had no idea what had happened to her mother and sister, but prayed they had made it out. Ryker held their escape against her, and eventually made good on his threat to force her to repent for it.

"You're going to be my wife," he told her. She could still remember that moment, the horror of it. Up until then, she had been almost committed to the Shepards, willing to do whatever it took to make sure they didn't go looking for her mother or sister. But that moment, after he uttered those words to River, it was too much. More than she knew she could ever handle.

She had to get out. She couldn't be his wife. Not in a million years. Even the thought of it was enough to make her feel sick. She swore to herself she would find a way out before she got married to that monster, and she started to plan her escape.

She paid attention to the rotation of people watching her, pocketed and stole stuff to hide for her travels when backs were turned, noted the distances from the different places she was working or sleeping to the nearest exits—hoping to escape into the woods and disappear.

One day, she found her opening. A couple of Ryker's men had started arguing and then a fight broke out and it captured everyone's attention, so she was momentarily forgotten.

She'd made her break for the woods and had been on the run since.

"That was the abusive ex you told me about?" Cade asked, as she filled him in on the story.

She nodded. "He was…rough with me," she replied, lowering her gaze to the ground. "But he was that way with everyone. He was worse than his father. More dangerous. More obsessive. And he's the one looking for me out there right now, I'm sure of it. He's the one hunting me."

"And you were going to your family?"

"Yes," she explained. "I know my mother has a lot of family in a small town in New York called Chittenango. That's where I'm headed. I need to find her and my sister again. I need to know they're okay…but you ruined it."

His eyes widened and he jerked back, dropping her hand. "What are you talking about?"

"You ruined it," she repeated, the lump in her throat making it hard to speak. "Because I… I couldn't risk caring about anyone, Cade. I couldn't risk getting sidetracked along the way. But now I'm here, and I… I really care about you! And I don't want to leave, even though I know I have to. Even though the Shepards are going to come looking for me, even though—"

Before she could say another word, he reached out and pulled her to him, planting his lips firmly against hers. She let out a surprised squeak, but then, closing her eyes, leaned into the kiss.

When he pulled back, he caught her face in his hands and looked deep into her eyes. The way he stared at her, it was like he was trying to see all the way into her soul. Her breath caught in her throat at the intensity of his gaze.

"You're safe here, River," he told her. "I'm going to make sure of that, you hear me?"

"Cade, you can't—"

"I can," he replied with conviction. "You don't know what I'm capable of. But I know I can protect you. Whatever it takes. And then, we'll get you back to your family, okay?"

She gazed at him for a long moment and, to her surprise, she found herself starting to relax. Even though she knew she should be terrified right now of what could happen, when he spoke those words to her, she believed him.

"Okay," she breathed back, and he kissed her again. And this time, she knew it was more than just a kiss. Now that she had laid herself bare to him, she wanted nothing more than to take their relationship to the next level.

To give herself to him utterly and completely.

Chapter Twenty-One

"Are you okay?" he murmured to her, tucking her hair back behind her ear as they lay next to each other in bed.

She nodded, leaning over to put her head on his chest. "Yeah," she whispered back. "I really am."

He smiled and wound his arms around her, pulling her in close. Being this intimate with her was a dream he'd never thought would come true. But the moment he had seen that desperate, helpless look in her eyes, he knew he had to take the chance to show her how much he meant it when he said he was going to protect her. She needed to know he was all in this with her.

Sleeping with her for the first time had been incredible, their bodies matching with each other as though it was the most natural thing in the world. And now, as they lay together in his bed, it was like the enormous weight of everything that had been holding them back was starting to drift away.

She had finally told him the truth, and though he could hardly wrap his head around the vastness of it, he was grateful that she had. It meant she finally trusted him completely. He could only imagine how hard it must've been for her to come clean to him like that. But it made everything about her just fall into place. All the questions that hadn't added up suddenly slotting together in a way he could make sense of. He was so glad he finally knew where she was coming from, even if it had been hard for her to tell him.

She had escaped from a cult. A damn cult. He couldn't imagine how painful it had been to lose her father like that, to be left behind by the rest of her family, and then having to rely on the people who had killed him to survive. And then to be told she was going to be married off to some psycho? From what he had heard about the Shepards, Ryker was a real piece of work, and the thought of him getting anywhere close to River was enough to make him feel sick.

He'd told River he would protect her and he meant it. He was going to do whatever it took to keep that promise. No one was going to lay a hand on her, not on his watch.

He smoothed his hand over her hair, letting his fingers drift down her back and follow the curve of her body. He was sure Lawson was waiting for him to return so he could fill him in on everything he had found out, but right now, he didn't want to break this moment. He didn't want to share her with anyone else. He wanted their time to last a little longer.

"So, now that you're going to be staying a while longer," he remarked. "Do you think you'll keep working on mending clothes, or see about doing something else?"

She smiled, snuggling into his chest. "I don't know," she replied. "I like sewing, it's what I know and I don't mind doing it. But also, I think I'd like to try something else. I was talking to Sarah, that therapist?"

"Yeah, I know her."

"Well, she said I could maybe help out with some of her

patients. Peer mentorship-type work," she replied, shaking her head. "It sounds crazy to me, but I...maybe I could help. It did feel nice to help that man the other day."

"Man?" he questioned. "What happened?"

She let out a small sigh that tickled the hair on his chest. "When I put my bag down to refill my water in the lodge, a new group of people were coming in and it made a loud bang noise when it hit the ground. It startled one of the men and he started having an episode. No one else was around, so I tried to talk him down. Bring him out of it. I felt so bad for causing him distress, but it felt really good to help a little." She shrugged and smiled into Cade's chest. "Anyway, Sarah was there and saw us and approached me about helping."

"That sounds amazing," he replied, stroking her hair. "I think you'd be really good at that."

"I don't know..."

"I do," he told her, and she smiled up at him.

It was clear it had been a long time since someone had actually talked to her like she was worth something. To give her praise or even a compliment. It killed him to think of how much she had been through already, knowing she never deserved anything that had happened to her. Cade wished he could take those burdens off her shoulders.

"Thanks," she murmured. "Maybe I'll take her up on it once things have calmed down. I'll think about it. That also will depend on if Lawson and Xavier will even let me stay here after this."

"You should," he urged her. "You would be a great help to her, I'd bet. And don't worry about the guys. Once they understand what's happened, they won't turn you away."

"I hope you're right. What about you?" she asked, turning the conversation to him once more.

"I'm going to help out with the squad, I think," he replied.

"The squad?"

"The one that Lawson runs," he explained. "It's a way for the guys who come here to get back on their feet and out into the field. They're helping out with the Feds' investigation into the Shepards right now."

"You think that's safe?" she asked, sounding fearful.

He squeezed her a little closer. "I know it is," he replied. "I can handle myself. And if it means taking down the group that has been causing you so much pain, it's not even something I have to think twice about."

She nodded but didn't reply. He knew she was worried and afraid, but it was something that he needed to do. He'd been trying to find his place, his new start since his injury, and this was the right fit for him. A way to keep his mind, body, and skills acquired through the years sharp. He also wanted her to know he meant what he said about her being safe and protected. And if he could use his skills and knowledge to help bring down the Shepards, that would be a bonus for them both.

Lying here with her in bed, he felt content for the first time in a long time. Even when he had been at peace before, he had always felt a hole inside him that never seemed to go away. He had been sure it was just because of his job—because of the life he'd left behind.

But when he was with her, all of that seemed to just fall away. Maybe it wasn't his work that he had needed, but a purpose. Something to drive him forward, even when things seemed impossible. And she was that purpose. Protecting her, making sure she had the life she needed and would never to have to fear for her safety or that of her family ever again.

Everything he had been looking and waiting for, it was lying in his arms at that moment. He couldn't imagine anything better, anything that would make him happier. His whole life had changed when he had suffered that injury, and he had thought it would be an uphill battle trying to get back to the point where he felt like a person again. But now, when he was with her, he had a purpose. He had a reason.

And it was River.

"I guess we should go talk to Lawson, huh?" River sighed.

Cade let out a groan. "No, let's just stay here," he replied. "I need to rest. And so do you. I'll talk to him in the morning."

She grinned and closed her eyes, hooking her leg over his. It was as though she couldn't get close enough to him.

He knew how she felt.

Even with their bodies pressed tightly against each other, he still wished they could be closer.

"I have to go to town with Hannah tomorrow," she murmured, smoothing a hand over his chest. "We have some supplies to pick up."

"I'm not sure that's a good idea. You think that'll be safe?" he asked. He could already feel himself starting to doze off, but he wanted to make sure she wasn't about to walk into the middle of a mess by heading off by herself.

"I hope so," she replied, and he ran his fingers through

her hair, pushing it back from her face. "We didn't have any problems and there's been no sighting in the town, right?"

"As far as I know, no, there hasn't. You'll be extra careful?" he asked her, and she nodded.

"I promise I will," she swore to him. "And Hannah too. We only have a few places to go, so it should quick. I don't think they'd try anything with a town full of people. There'll be plenty of people around while we're there."

"Stay close to populated areas, and don't go off on your own for any reason. It's not going to be long until we have Ryker and his gang behind bars," he promised her. "Soon you won't have to worry at all."

"I hope so."

"You don't have to hope," he replied. "I'll make it happen, River. Just watch me."

She smiled as her eyes drifted shut.

He stayed awake until he was sure she had dozed off to sleep, and then let himself drift off as well. When he fell asleep with her in his arms, he was even more sure than ever of what he had to do next.

Whatever it took to keep her safe. And whatever she needed to have the future she deserved.

Chapter Twenty-Two

River glanced around as she and Hannah stepped out of the truck, suddenly feeling like eyes were on her. She knew she was being paranoid after everything that had happened and how close the Shepards seemed to be. She couldn't help it, though. She was second-guessing everything about being here without Cade, or even one of the other men from the lodge. She'd had a large knot in her stomach since she'd gotten up this morning.

Hannah knew what was happening, but didn't seem to let it be diminishing her normal bright and cheerful disposition. Or maybe she was just trying to help River feel more comfortable. Either way, River just wanted to try to enjoy spending time with her friend.

"Thanks for coming into town with me today," she remarked, hooking one of the reusable totes that River had made for them over her shoulder. "It's so much more fun with some company, isn't it?"

"Yeah, exactly," River agreed, but in truth, she was more than a little nervous about being out in the open like this, regardless of what she'd told Cade yesterday. She had promised Hannah she would come to town with her to help her pick up her stuff since Hannah didn't want to ask one of the guys. Apparently, her brother and Xavier were still only barely talking and she didn't like the thought of her friend being stuck between them, so River had volunteered. But there was a part of her that was fearful the Shepards might swoop in as soon as they got the chance.

But she couldn't let the fear of them get in the way of her living her life, she knew that much. Besides, Cade had sworn to her the night before that he wasn't going to let anything happen to her.

And she believed him, she really did. The way that he spoke, it was as though he had never been surer of anything in his entire life. She trusted that—trusted him. He had a long history in the military, and he had taken a serious injury as part of his service. If anyone could take whatever the Shepards and Ryker threw at him, it would be Cade.

"You want to get some breakfast first?" Hannah suggested, gesturing to the small diner sitting just off the square.

River grinned and nodded. "Sure. That sounds great," she agreed.

They headed to grab a spot at one of the booths on the far side of the diner. Hannah insisted that River try the waffles, and the two of them tucked into a steaming plate of syrupy breakfast as the rain began to fall outside.

"Wow, that's good," River murmured.

Hannah grinned. "I told you so," she replied proudly. "So, what's on your mind? You've been a little quiet today. More quiet than normal, I mean."

"I, uh…" she began. She didn't want to tell Hannah the truth about her past. The fewer people that knew, the better it would be for her. Plus, she didn't want to get into all the details in a place so public or take more time than necessary to get the supplies. She just wanted to help Hannah get what was needed and return to the lodge…to Cade. But she had to give her something.

"I'm thinking about what I'm going to do at the lodge when I've finished with all the clothes and supplies," she replied.

"Oh, yeah? You got something in mind?"

"Sarah said I could maybe help her out in some way with the therapy," she replied. "I don't know if I would actually be any good, but…"

"I bet you would be," Hannah replied encouragingly. "You're always a really good listener, River. You would do a great job with that. Have you ever thought about becoming a therapist?"

"I—I guess I could train." River shrugged, raising her eyebrows as the thought of it crossed her mind.

She had never really thought much about what life might look like for her down the road, after the Shepards. But after her conversation with Cade, realizing she wanted to stay there at the lodge, she might need to start. She could actually think about what she wanted to do with her future. And maybe she could help others with the knowledge she had gained from her own suffering.

She and Hannah continued with their meals and chatted about the possibility of her working with Sarah. For the first time in too long, River felt really hopeful. Like there was a future beyond what she had imagined for herself. She wasn't going to be trapped in a marriage with Ryker. She was free—and that freedom was almost dizzying as she tried to wrap her head around it.

"Okay, I guess we should actually get going and get the errands done since we're finished here," Hannah said, once they both cleaned their plates. "Come on, I left the lodge business credit card in the truck. Let's grab it and finish up so we can get back."

River wholeheartedly agreed. They had already wasted enough time stopping to eat, though it was really good and the food had actually helped settle some of her nerves a bit.

She followed Hannah out of the diner, and she had a smile on her face as they walked back to the truck. Her mind kept wandering to her future—to a future she had hardly dared imagine for herself before, but that now seemed within her grasp. And that future was more tempting than anything in the world. A future she got to choose for herself—maybe a future with Cade too.

But before her mind could stray any further down that path, a car screeched to a halt beside them. River spun around, her eyes wide as panic gripped her. A moment later, a man leaped out of the car and slammed a rag over her mouth.

"River!" Hannah screamed, and it was the last thing River heard before the blackness swallowed her up completely.

When River came to, her head was throbbing with pain. In fact, her whole body ached. Her head had sunk down to her chest, and she lifted it and looked around. She couldn't see anything, couldn't even remember how she had gotten here. She went to lift her hand to brush her hair back from her face, but she couldn't move. Something bit into her arms, pinning them in place.

She let out a whimper as the memory of what had happened before she blacked out rose up in her mind. They had gotten her. She didn't know how they had found her, but as soon as she had felt that rough fabric over her mouth and the thick, chemical scent of a sedative filled her nostrils, she had known it. And now she was here—God only knew where this place was—and she didn't know if she was ever going to be able to get out.

"She's awake."

A light flicked on, hurting River's eyes. She looked around the space again as her eyes adjusted to see if she could figure out where she was. She was restrained in an old, rickety wooden chair with zip ties, the plastic digging painfully into her skin. Her mouth was dry and her stomach twisted and turned inside of her. How long had she been here? She wasn't even sure she wanted to know the answer to that question.

"Good to see you again, River."

Everything in her froze when she heard that voice. The voice of her nightmares. Her ears suddenly started ringing so loud she thought she'd go deaf. Her heart pounded painfully in her chest and her muscles seized as if they would snap apart. She turned her head toward the voice, and there he was. The very last person she ever wanted to see again.

Ryker.

His hair had grown out slightly, hanging in a shaggy mess to his shoulders, and his clothes were dirty and ragged. His wolf-like eyes cut through her, and that predatory grin spread over his face. The combination was startling and chilled her to the bone.

"You miss me?" he asked her, reaching out to cup her

chin tightly in his hand. She tried to pull her face away, but his grip was too strong. Being this close to him again after the past few months on the run was enough to turn her stomach.

No. She couldn't do this. Not again. She couldn't have gotten so far from him just to end up back in his grasp. She should never have left the safety of the lodge. She was so stupid to believe she'd actually escaped him when she knew, she *knew*, there was no way. Ryker would never let her go.

She lowered her eyes to the ground. She wasn't going to give him her attention, no matter how much he seemed to think he was entitled to it. No matter how much he wanted it.

"You've been out for six hours, sweetheart," he continued, letting go of her face, though she could still feel the grip of his finger on her jaw.

Six hours? Her heart sank. Cade. What was going through his mind? Would he be looking for her? How would he even find her? She prayed he wouldn't give up on her.

And Hannah! What had happened to Hannah? She had been with her when River was abducted. What if something had happened to her? What if she had been hurt, or worse?

She wanted to ask the questions but she couldn't get her mouth to form the words. Was afraid of the answers she'd get if she did. She couldn't bear it if something happened to one of her friends because of her.

"Don't worry, River," Ryker continued. "We're going to get you back home. Back where you belong, right?"

River tensed but didn't say a word to him. She knew he would twist up anything she said and use it against her. He would find some way to make it seem like she had agreed to go back with him, even though they both knew she'd never willingly go back. Especially not with him.

Before he could continue, another man stepped into the small room with them. It looked like an old hunting cabin or something, paint peeling off the walls and old cans of food stacked in the cabinets with doors that seemed to be half hanging off their hinges.

"We need to move, boss," the man told him.

River recognized him—one of her father's friends. She wanted to scream at him, ask him if this was what her father would have wanted him to do. What would he have thought if he had been able to see this man, a friend of his, involved in the kidnapping of his daughter? He couldn't even make eye contact with River, and it didn't surprise her. He knew what he was doing was twisted and wrong.

Ryker let out a snarl of irritation. "You should never have let that other girl get away," he snapped at the other man.

The other girl? Hannah? She had managed to get away? River felt a flood of relief hit her. *Thank God.*

"And now she's going to bring the pigs to our door," he continued. "Get everyone together, tell them we're ready to move out."

Move out? Move out where? River glanced between the men, trying to pick up on anything she could, but it was no good. They weren't interested in dealing with her right now; they were intent on doing whatever they could to make sure they didn't get caught.

Ryker flipped out a knife and cut the bindings tying her to the chair before yanking her up with a hard jerk that rattled her teeth. Before she could protest, he had her arms gripped in front of her and fastened more ties around her wrists. She felt a cold chill whipping in from outside, and she wished she had Cade's winter coat with her—something to keep her warm, and something to remind her of him.

"Come on. Move," Ryker ordered, and he dragged her toward the door of the cabin. His grip was tight and unyielding. She tried to pull herself away, but he hung on even tighter. He wasn't letting her go anywhere now that he had her where he wanted her.

Outside, it had started to snow just the slightest bit. There was maybe half an inch lying on the well-trodden ground and it was still coming down. That was going to make it harder for them to find her, or even a trail.

But as she stumbled behind Ryker, who was dragging her roughly through the dense woods, she had to trust that Cade meant it when he said he could protect her. No matter how easy it would have been to let her fear and doubt get the better of her, she was going to trust in him until she was given a reason not to.

Because right now, he was her only chance of getting out of here in one piece.

Chapter Twenty-Three

"What the hell do we do now?"

"Cade, I know this is tough for you, but—"

"Tough?" Cade exploded at Carter. He knew it wasn't going to do him any good to be mean to the people around him, but he felt like he was going crazy. He'd felt like this ever since Hannah had rushed back from their trip to town to tell them that some men had snatched up River off the street and she had no idea where they had taken her.

He'd never forget the look of panic and fear on Hannah's face when she'd burst into their meeting in Lawson's office to tell them what happened.

After kissing River goodbye at their cabin, Cade had called Lawson to see if he and Xavier were available to talk about River's past with the Shepards. Lawson was still miffed that Cade had never gotten back to him the night before but agreed that he and Xavier would meet him in Lawson's office to discuss the specifics and make a plan for what came next. Cade had barely finished telling them what River told him before Hannah had exploded into the office.

"She could be anywhere!" Cade continued as Xavier got to his feet to try and calm him. "It's been hours. Where the hell is she?"

"We're doing everything we can to find out," Lawson reminded him as Cade began to pace once more. "We've got guys out doing another patrol of the woods."

"She's not in the woods," he muttered, shaking his head. "They couldn't have gotten their cars up there, it's too dense."

"Well, they didn't take the roads, either," Carter reminded him. "There are police stationed on every road in and out of this place. They've been there since she was taken. They couldn't have gotten past them. So she can't have gone far. The woods are the best bet."

Cade rubbed a hand over his face, trying to settle his scattered thoughts. He knew he couldn't let himself spin out of control like this, but it felt like it had been an eternity since River had been taken, not just hours. He was terrified at the thought of what the Shepards could be doing to her.

If she was even still alive.

The moment Hannah had finished detailing what had happened in town, they had all launched into action. Calls were made to send out guys to patrol the area, including searching close to town, and alert the local police. Cade hadn't left out any detail of what River had shared with him about her past in hopes that the smallest thing might give them a leg up in tracking her down. But so far, nothing. No sign of her, or any of the Shepards, either. What had they done to her? Where had they taken her?

"So, what's our next move?" he demanded.

Cade couldn't just sit around and do nothing. He had to get out there and help. He had to hope they were right when they said she couldn't have been taken too far from the lodge. But even the distance between them right now was more than he could take. He had promised to protect her, and now she was out there, trapped in the middle of a nightmare he couldn't pull her out of.

"We have some thermal imaging cameras," Xavier suggested. "We could set up a camp at the edge of the forest and send out a couple of drones to see if we can find any people out there. Should be easier than normal because of the snow."

The snow. Cade had been trying not to think about that part. He hated the thought of her out there in the snow, freezing and lost and wondering if anyone was coming to find her. He prayed she knew that he was coming for her, no matter what. He wouldn't stop searching until he found out where she was.

"What are we waiting for?" he demanded again. "I'm getting the guys together to set it up now."

"I'll come with you," Xavier replied, getting to his feet. They were in the main office, and Cade couldn't sit around any longer. He had to do something. Xavier had seemed just as invested as him, and Cade wondered if it had something to do with how close Hannah had come to getting snatched up too.

"Okay, good," Cade replied. "Let's go."

They grabbed a few more guys and everything they needed and packed into the truck. Cade insisted on driving, even though the cold had his shoulder aching more than usual. He needed to take control of something, needed to drive this thing forward in any way he could.

He was already cursing himself for letting her go without him by her side. They never would have gotten to her if he had been the one with her in town. But it was too late to worry about that now. What mattered was getting her back.

At the east edge of the forest, the guys unpacked the supplies and began to set up the drones. Cade paced back and forth, feet crunching in the snow, wondering if they could go any faster.

"How long is this going to take?" he muttered to Xavier.

"Not long," Xavier assured him. "You just have to wait a little longer. We'll find her."

"We have to," Cade replied. And then, he heard something—the crack of a footstep on the snow in the woods.

His head snapped up. "What was that?" he demanded.

"I didn't hear anything," Xavier replied, but Cade grabbed one of the flashlights and shined it into the woods. It bounced off the shadows, and then he saw it—a man darting back into the trees.

"There! There's someone there!" he yelled, and he took off after him. The man was winding in and out of the trees, trying to vanish back into the darkness, but Cade wasn't going to let him get away. His eyes were pinned on his target as he cut in and out of the branches around him, feet crunching on the compacted snow beneath him, until he was within grabbing distance.

He threw himself at the man, wrapping his arms around his waist and tackling him to the ground with a sharp thud. The man tried to scramble away, but Cade held on tight. Soon enough, Xavier and a couple of the other guys appeared through the trees to help.

"Get him back to base," Cade spat, pulling the man upright and shoving him toward the other men. They dragged him back through the woods toward the truck, where a couple of the lodge's men were setting up the thermal drones.

"Who the hell are you?" Cade demanded, shoving the man back against the side of the truck, fisting his collar in his hands. The man wore the same ragged clothing River had worn when she first met her, and he knew at once he had to be part of the Shepards.

"Let me go," the man muttered as he struggled in Cade's grasp.

Cade narrowed his eyes at him. "What are you doing out here?"

"It's a free country, I was just hunting—"

"Not without a permit, you weren't," he shot back. "Tell me what you're doing here. Are you with the Shepards?"

The man's eyes widened in surprise, but he did his best to cover it up.

"Who's that?" he asked. "I've never heard of them—"

"Don't you lie to me," Cade snarled. "You're with the Shepards, aren't you?"

"I told you, I don't—"

"You can tell us, or you can tell it to the cops," he added. "How does that sound? I think they're going to have some big questions for you."

Cade slammed his fist into the panel next to the man's head, and the guy jerked in surprise. Cade needed him to know how far he would take this. He would do whatever it took to get River back, and he knew this man had the information he needed.

"We're sending out a drone over that forest, so we're going to find your psycho little cult one way or another," he told him. "Better for you to tell us where we should look.

Or do you want to talk to the cops about this?" He took a step back, waiting. "Talk!"

The man's expression shifted. Cade could tell by the look on his face he was trying to think of what best to say. Cade glared at him with clenched fists, waiting for him to break—and then, at last, he did.

"They were staying in a hunting lodge on the north side of the forest," he grumbled, eyes lowering to the ground as though he couldn't believe he was really admitting it.

"Over to the north of the forest!" Cade yelled to the guys programming the drone. "Get it out there, now!"

He zip-tied the man's hands and shoved him into the truck, locking the doors to make sure he couldn't go anywhere. He was sure he could get some more information out of him when the time was right. Even if he couldn't, the Feds would have plenty to say to him about his involvement with the Shepards. But right now, he had one goal in mind, and he needed to find out where River was before the Shepards could get out of there.

They launched the drones, and Cade paced back and forth, shooting glances at the screen where the thermal imaging cameras were broadcasting.

"There! There's something," Xavier exclaimed, jabbing his finger at the picture. Sure enough, a cluster of heat spots stood out on the screen.

"It looks like a lot of people," the man running the drone remarked. "Could be the whole group making a break for it."

"What's that?" Cade demanded, gesturing to a couple of smaller spots breaking off from the main group.

"Looks like there's a smaller group splitting from them," he replied, frowning. "Two people, from the looks of it."

Two people. Cade's head spun as he tried to come up with a plan. Two people—Ryker and River, he was sure of it. Even if the rest of the gang were on the run, he was out there doing his best to capture her and keep her to himself.

"I'm going after them," Cade announced.

Xavier grabbed his arm. "Cade, no," he warned. "We need to put some backup together. You can't just go off after them like that—"

"Watch me," Cade snapped back, yanking his arm loose. There was no way he was going to let Ryker get any farther with her than he already had. He was going to catch him and bring her back. He was going to take him down, once and for all. And River was going to be safe.

He couldn't wait any longer. He sprinted off into the woods, Xavier's shouts fading behind him, and rushed toward the woman he loved.

Chapter Twenty-Four

She stumbled behind Ryker, doing whatever she could to stay upright as he dragged her through the freezing woods. She heard a commotion through the trees, but she wasn't sure what was going on. The whole forest seemed to be alive with people rushing around, calling to each other, but she couldn't figure out why. Had someone found them? She could only hope they had.

"Hurry up, bitch!" Ryker spat at her, and she did her best to match his pace, but her body was aching from the cold and the bindings. She couldn't keep up.

"Slow down," she protested.

He spun around and lashed out so fast she had no time to react. She started falling back and he reached out and yanked her to his chest, his eyes flashing with anger. "You don't get to tell me what to do," he snapped. "Not after all the crap you've put me through."

River wanted to protest, but she was sure there was no point. He was in a rage and there would be no reasoning with him. He'd already decided it was all her fault, when he was the one responsible for this nightmare. If Ryker had just let her go and not followed her, none of this would be happening. But no, he had decided that he was owed something from her, and he wasn't going to stop until he got it.

He wasn't going to stop until she was tied to him for life.

"I didn't want any of this, Ryker!" she protested, hoping she could get through to him somehow. He reached out again, grabbing her arm, pulling her forward. She mustered up all the strength and confidence she could as she tracked in his footsteps. If she got lost in this forest she likely wouldn't survive.

"You made your vows to the Shepards like everyone else," he reminded her.

"You think I wanted to make those vows?" she demanded. "I was a child. I was forced to! You would have hurt my family. And it didn't protect my father, did it? He's dead!"

"He's dead because he tried to walk away from everything my father gave to him," he snarled back at her, his voice dripping with venom. "He owed us. If he hadn't been a coward—"

"Don't you call him that," she snapped, her voice colder than she had ever heard it. Her ability to speak to him like that surprised her, but she had put up with enough. Her father was a strong man, stronger than so many of the people who had been nothing but cowards. People who were willing to go along with what the Shepards demanded from them. They could see the evil that was being done, the harm they were causing, but they allowed themselves and their families to remain a part of it because they were terrified of the retribution.

Well, not her father. He had tried to get them out. And, in the case of Haven and her mother, he had succeeded.

River just needed to find a way to leave this all behind, and she would have fulfilled his last wish.

He spun around to face her and drew his hand back, landing a sharp slap on her face. She gasped at the pain, her head reeling.

"I'll call him whatever I want," he sneered at her. "Come on. We've got to get to the meeting point. Then we can get out of here."

Get out of here? River slowed, trying to pull him back, but he grabbed the ties still binding her hands and yanked her forward.

"Don't think you're getting out of it that easy. I'll get what I'm owed yet," he told her, and dragged her onward.

"How did you find me?" she suddenly asked, tripping over her own feet trying to keep up with him. Maybe if she could slow Ryker down some, she could try to make an escape.

He stopped suddenly and River almost ran into his back. He turned with a scowl on his face and she was almost sorry she'd asked the question, but she really wanted to know.

"I've been looking for you since you pulled your stunt and took off. I've had the guys branching out in all directions since we left home searching in every hidey-hole along the way. Just so happened a couple of the guys decided to stop by that lodge where you've been staying and thought they recognized you. Since we hit a warehouse not too far from here, I decided to stop in for a look. We've been keeping an eye on you since, looking for an opportunity to get you back without one of those men around you."

River's eyes widened at his reply. They'd been watching her, so she'd never been safe like she'd thought. She couldn't stop the horrible what ifs running through her mind. Thank goodness they'd just waited to take her away from the lodge instead of doing something more violent. If they'd attacked the others to get to her, she would have never forgiven herself.

He quickly turned and jerked her forward again. She did her best to follow him, but she was so cold, the freezing air clinging to her skin and making her shiver hard. Ryker looked at her, shaking his head as though he couldn't believe what he was seeing.

"You're getting soft, River," he scoffed. "But don't worry, we'll get you hardened back up once we get back to base. I can't have a weakling as my wife. How will you raise our children if you can't even stand a little cold?"

River's teeth chattered too hard to reply, but her mind registered the horror of what he'd just said. Their children? She couldn't imagine having kids with this monster. She couldn't even imagine him touching her without feeling ill.

He continued to pull her along behind him and she felt like a yo-yo. She was beyond frozen and her body was becoming so stiff she didn't know how much longer she could go on. Not that Ryker cared about her well-being. He just kept yanking her behind him until all at once, her foot caught on a rock. Unable to brace herself, she toppled forward and crashed down on the ground, bringing him with her.

"Damn it!" he exclaimed. For a split second, he let go of her. River's mind raced—she had to take this chance. She might not get one again. If he got her to the meeting spot and managed to haul her out of here, she would never see anyone from the lodge again.

She forced herself up as quickly as she could manage and willed her body to move, darting off into the woods, her breath tearing from her lungs in huge gasps. She heard Ryker screaming after her, but she didn't dare turn around to see where he was. She had to put as much distance between herself and that man as she—

Suddenly, the earth dropped away in front of her, and she came to a sharp halt. She was next to a drop-off that led down a steep slope to the frozen river below. She was trapped! She had nowhere to go. She could hear Ryker slashing through the trees, his heavy footsteps getting closer. She looked around frantically and spotted a large, jagged rock sticking out from the snow. With her frozen fingers, she tugged it out of its spot, clutching it in her closed hands. It was the closest thing she had to a weapon right now.

"There you are."

Her heart stopped when she heard Ryker's taunting voice. Spinning around, she found him standing a few feet away from her, with a maniacal grin on his face.

"I'll jump!" she threatened him.

He shook his head. "I don't think you have the nerve," he replied calmly, and he reached under his shirt and pulled out a gun. River stared at the black barrel aimed at her and wondered if this was similar to the last moments of her father's life before he was murdered.

"Go on, then, jump," he told her, motioning to the cliff's edge with the gun. Her foot skidded back slightly, and she looked down toward the water. It was frozen solid. The drop alone would break her legs, or worse.

"That's what I thought," he remarked, taking another

step toward her, his feet crunching on the snow as he drew closer to her…and closer still. Her heart sank and she realized this was it. She couldn't escape, there was nowhere to run. The only way she could survive was to willingly go with him. But if she did that, she feared she would never see the lodge—or her friends—ever again. And Cade…

She gripped the rock tighter, wondering if she had it in her to fight him off. He was almost on top of her now, and she stepped back on instinct, her heel skidding over the sharp drop to the openness below. She felt the world shrinking around her as Ryker took the final steps to stop in front of her, and she knew this was it. No more running, no more trying to escape. This next moment would determine if she'd live or die.

Would Ryker grab her and force her to their next destination or would he finally decide she's been enough trouble and kill her where she stood?

Either way, it was over.

Then she saw it. A slight movement in the woods behind him. Her lips parted, her eyes widened, and her heart leaped when she realized who it was.

"Cade," she breathed.

"What?" Ryker demanded, and he spun around to see where she was looking.

Everything seemed to move in slow motion for a moment while she debated what to do. The rock was still in her hand, and she was close enough now to take a swing. If she was going to do this, she had to do it now.

She lifted the rock above her head with both tied hands, and used the momentum to bring it down with a sickening crack into the side of Ryker's head.

He fell like a stone to the ground, not even making a sound as he dropped. River's eyes widened and she gasped. The rock slipped out of her fingers. Had she killed him? His eyes were blank and vacant, the same way her father's had been when she had seen him laid out on the ground of their driveway.

Cade rushed toward her and pulled her into his arms.

"Hey, hey, I've got you," he murmured, and quickly removed the bindings from her wrists before he gently took her face into his hands.

River knew she should say something, acknowledge Cade in some way. But she couldn't take her eyes off Ryker's body on the ground, unmoving. *Dead.* Before she could stop herself, she let out a wail of shock, the sound bouncing off the trees as she tried to wrap her head around what she had just done.

"Are you okay?" Concern laced his words as he waited for her to answer. She still couldn't look away from the body. Cade leaned forward and kissed her forehead before wrapping her in his jacket and trying to move her away from the scene.

She felt like she was floating outside her body and had to force her feet to move. She was shaking so hard from the cold, she thought she'd crumble into pieces.

"Let's get you out of here," he told her, and leaned down to check on Ryker's body before he led her away from the clearing. She was crying, her body wracked by enormous sobs that she couldn't control. Cade pulled her closer to his side and continued walking them away.

Once he had gotten her out of the clearing, he paused to let her catch her breath.

"Are you hurt?" he asked, looking her over.

She couldn't say anything. She couldn't even breathe right now. Had she killed him? She'd killed him, right? She saw him lying on the ground, empty eyes looking up. He was dead. He had to be. Was it…over?

Cade checked her for injuries, and she let him. She couldn't react to anything he was saying. Her body was in lockdown, both shock from the cold and the adrenaline leaving her system. His hands were strong and sure as they moved over her, and she wondered how she could have done that. Had she had that in her all along? Was she really capable of it? Killing someone? Why hadn't she done it before? He really was gone, right? Dead. So many thoughts. Too many questions. It was suddenly too loud in her mind, but silence surrounded them.

Finally, she was able to speak again.

"Is he dead?" she croaked, her voice sounding broken. It had started to snow even harder, the cold closing in around them. She knew they couldn't stay out here much longer, but she needed to know for sure.

Cade nodded. "He is, River. He is," he assured her. "There was no pulse. You killed him, River. It's over. It's really over."

She felt her legs turn to mush and heard Cade's startled "umph" as she collapsed into him. How long had she been waiting to hear those words? She couldn't believe it. Ryker was dead, just like his father. There was nobody to lead the Shepards anymore.

She couldn't believe it was really true. Ryker was gone. His followers had no leader. He was lying dead in the woods while they were all trying to run away. No one knew. She wanted to laugh out loud, or scream, or...something. Her emotions were scattered all over the place.

She kept replaying the moment where she swung the rock at his head, the feel of it thud against his skull, even the sickening cracking sound. Seeing him fall lifeless to the ground. His dead eyes. She'd done that.

"Let's get you out of here," Cade told her. "You need to get warm and we need to get you checked out for real."

She shook her head and her eyes suddenly felt heavy. She felt like she was wading through mud. It must be the adrenaline crash. Cade seemed to realize this and stopped to pick her up.

"No, I need to walk on my own. I can do it," she said more confidently than she felt at the moment.

Cade nodded and wrapped his arm around her again to steady her. He seemed to know where he was going, so she allowed him to guide her through the trees. It was a relief to rely on him because all of these trees looked the same to her. She'd get turned around in a heartbeat, especially in the state she was in now. She trusted him to get her to safety.

She might have been dragged into this forest as a victim, as just another one of the dozens of people the Shepards had hurt over the years, but she wasn't walking out of it as one. She had finally done it. She'd stood up to Ryker and finally ended his reign of terror. She was free.

The elated feeling was almost more than she could take, and she nearly felt drunk on it, knowing she had freed herself and her mother and her sister and many others from the clutches of a man as evil as Ryker. But she also felt guilty, knowing she had taken a life, even if he had been a monster.

She clung on to Cade for dear life, and kept her eyes

fixed ahead of her. She didn't know what she was going to do now that she didn't have to run anymore. One thing she was sure of, though—whatever came next, she could handle it.

Chapter Twenty-Five

Cade lifted his hand to try and keep the snow off his face. The blizzard was really starting to set in now, and he wasn't sure how much longer they would be able to make it out here in the cold.

River wasn't saying anything, but that didn't surprise him. God knew what they had done to her since the last time he had seen her. He would get to the bottom of it once they were safe again, but right now, all he wanted was to get her back to the lodge and make sure she was okay.

He couldn't believe he had found her. His instincts had been right—the two people breaking away from the larger group were Ryker and River. Cade didn't know where Ryker had been planning to take her, but he was glad he had managed to get to them in time. She seemed to have broken free from Ryker's grasp, at least for long enough to put some distance between them, but Ryker had trained a gun on her by the time he reached them.

"It's okay, it's okay," he told her over and over again, as he guided her through the forest and back to the freedom waiting for her beyond. He still couldn't believe what he had seen, but he should have known she was capable of something like that—of showing that strength. She had fought so hard to get away from the Shepards, and she had proven herself willing to do anything to make sure she never had to go back.

All at once, he spotted Xavier in the woods, weaving in and out of the trees along with a few of the other guys from the lodge.

"Cade!" he yelled out.

Cade lifted a hand to acknowledge him. "How far are we from the truck?" he called back.

"A few minutes," Xavier replied, and he glanced over at River. "What happened? Is she okay?"

"I'll tell you once we get back," he replied. "I need to get her to the lodge and out of the cold. And she needs to get checked out. I want to see if they've done anything to her."

"Right," Xavier agreed, and he looped an arm around her waist and helped Cade carry her the rest of the way back through the forest. Cade knew from the heavier snowfall and the cutting feel of the wind that it must be below freezing by now, but he could hardly feel it. The only thing he felt was her, and the only thing he could think about was getting her back to safety as fast as possible.

The guys around them spread out to fill the woods, probably planning on catching the rest of the Shepards who had scattered earlier. They wouldn't get far, not in this weather. And when they found out that their leader was dead, they would surely give up once and for all.

Finally, Xavier, Cade and River broke the tree line, and Cade found himself opposite the truck once more. The guys had set up a makeshift tent to hold off the weather, and he noticed a few medical personnel inside. Cade rushed River toward it.

"I need someone to check her over," he told them, not speaking to anyone in particular. He didn't care who helped him with this, he just needed to make certain she was all right.

"Okay, bring her in the tent," one of the medics, Lawrence, instructed him. "I'll take a quick look at her so we've got an idea of what we're dealing with."

A couple of guys with Lawrence approached and Cade turned River over to them and watched as she was guided into the tent. Cade stopped and took a deep breath, pulling the cold air into his lungs, and Xavier finally followed up on his earlier question.

"So," he asked, as Lawson emerged from the truck to join them. "You going to tell us what happened out there?"

"I was right—the two people separated on the heat sensor were Ryker and River," he explained, sighing. "When I got to them, she was standing at the edge of the cliff and he had a gun on her. I thought she was going to jump to get away from him."

"Damn," Lawson muttered, glancing over at the tent where River disappeared.

"But he…when he heard me coming, he took his attention off her for a second, and she hit him with this huge rock she had hidden in her hands," Cade continued. "He's dead. Ryker is dead."

The two fell silent for a moment, clearly stunned by what they heard. Cade couldn't blame them. Looking at River now, it was hard to believe she would have been capable of something like that just a little while ago.

"Is she going to get in any kind of trouble for it?" Cade

asked, lowering his voice. If he had to cover for her, hide the truth of what she had done, he would.

Lawson shook his head. "I doubt it," he replied. "After everything she's been through with that guy, I can't imagine anyone is going to bother pressing charges. They'll just be glad to get rid of him."

Cade nodded in relief. He had thought as much, but with River having been part of the Shepards in the past, he wasn't certain that they would be so quick to let her walk away from this without some kind of pushback. He hoped she'd be free and clear of it all.

"Where are the rest of the Shepards?" he asked.

"We've got our guys tracking them down in the forest," Xavier explained. "Once they figure out their leader is done for, I think it's going to be a hell of a lot easier. They'll give up. They won't know what to do with themselves when they find out he's not there to call the shots anymore."

Cade closed his eyes and rubbed a hand over his face. He was exhausted, but it was only really just hitting him that she was safe. She was going to be okay, and he couldn't think of anything else that mattered right now. Even if there were still Shepards out there, he had managed to get her out—no, *she* had managed to get herself out. She had fought and found a way to freedom, despite everything she had been through. He just hoped she hadn't been hurt in the process.

"Go check on your woman, Cade. The rest can wait," Lawson directed. "There's nothing you need to do now but get her home and take care of her."

"And rest," Xavier added.

"You sure?" Cade asked. "I can stick around, help with rounding up the rest of the Shepards—"

"No way," Lawson replied as he shook his head. "You've done enough. You need to get her back home and warmed up."

"Thanks, guys," Cade replied, and turned toward the tent.

He noticed there were more vehicles around, including law enforcement, as he approached the tent where Lawrence was checking her over. This area was going to be active for a while, and tonight's activities were going to be the talk of the town and the lodge come morning.

Cade saw one of the men from the lodge pointing a couple of officers in the direction of the tent and he picked up his pace to get there first. Lawrence noticed his approach and walked out to meet him and fill him in on River's condition.

"She looks as though she's mostly fine," Lawrence confirmed. "She's got a bruise forming on her face from where she said he hit her, her wrists are a bit raw from the bindings, and she's got a few bumps and other bruises from being taken and dragged around. Nothing that won't heal. The big thing is the cold. You got her back here before it turned critical, but she'll need to get warm as soon as possible, and a hot meal wouldn't hurt, either."

Cade glanced over his shoulder to see how close the officers were and watched as Lawson went to intercept them.

Cade breathed a sigh of relief. All he wanted to do now was get her back to their cabin, see for himself that she was okay, get her warmed up, and then sleep for a week. Everything else could wait. After the range of emotions he'd experienced in the last several hours, he was beyond exhausted, and he could only imagine how River was feeling since she'd been through so much more.

"Cade, before you go, these officers need a statement from you and River," Lawson said with a frown, clearly not happy that they were being detained. "I asked them to wait until later so you could both rest, but they said it had to be done now. Sorry, man." He shook his head and stepped to the side as two officers took his place.

"Hello. I'm Officer Baker and this is my partner, Officer Dobbs. We need a few questions answered before you go," one of them said in a polite but firm voice.

"Later, man. Go as soon as you can." Lawson clapped Cade on the shoulder, then walked back in the direction of Xavier and the others. Cade motioned for the officers to follow him into the tent.

River looked so small sitting in one of the chairs where Lawrence had left her. Someone had given her a couple of blankets and she was so wrapped up you could hardly see her beneath them. She saw him approach and stood to meet him, a wariness in her gaze as she noticed the officers behind him.

"We're going home?" River asked in a quiet voice, as she leaned up against him. Her shivering seemed to have abated some, and her skin didn't feel as cold, but she clutched on to him like she was hanging on for dear life.

"Yeah, soon," Cade murmured to her, pressing a kiss on the top of her head. "We have to give our statements, then we can go."

"Am I in trouble?" she whispered into Cade's chest, her eyes slightly wide.

"You're going to be fine," he assured her and pulled her firmly to his side. "I promise. We'll be out of here soon."

One of the officers stepped closer and River startled. "Sorry, ma'am. We need to ask a few questions, like Mr. Thatcher said, then you'll be free to go." Officer Dobbs offered her a friendly smile and pulled out a notepad. "Shall we sit?" He directed them back to the chairs.

Cade listened as River told the officers everything that had happened. He was so proud of her. Her voice held strength and confidence as she recalled every detail with Ryker, even going back to her father's death and her running and ending up at the lodge.

The few questions had turned into an interview that took an hour and a half, and River was fading. Her words were sounding like mere whispers when Cade finally put a stop to it all. "Guys, I need to get her home. If you have more questions, you can reach us at the lodge in a couple of days. She won't be available until then." Giving the officers no time to respond, Cade whisked her up in his arms and carried her out to the truck.

Carter appeared as he was tucking River into the seat and offered to drive them back to the cabin. Given how tired he was, he wasn't going to turn down the offer. Any chance he had to just be with River without having to worry about anything else, he would take.

He climbed in and River cuddled into him. He draped an arm around her, pulling her in closer to share some of his body heat with her.

"I'm so glad you're okay," he murmured to her.

She looked up at him, biting her lip. "Do you really think everything's okay?"

"You did what you had to do, River. No one will fault you for that. And if it hadn't been you, it would have been someone else. You just saved the authorities the trouble of having to take him in."

"You think so?"

"I know so," Cade promised her, and she rested her head on his chest, seemingly satisfied by his answer. He ran his fingers through her hair, and watched as she drifted off to sleep against him.

Soon enough, he found himself following her. He felt his body relax for the first time since he found out she was taken. He wasn't sure what was going to happen next with the investigation or the Shepards still on the loose, but at least she was back with him and safe.

She was the only thing that mattered to him, and he was amazed by her at every turn—her bravery, her strength, her willingness to fight for herself. Even faced with one of the most formidable criminals in the country, she hadn't let him get the best of her. No, she had stood up for herself and fought back.

And now she was calling the lodge home. It was home for Cade, had been for a while, and he was so glad she was starting to see it the same way he did. He hoped it would be a while before she decided to start on her way again.

Slowly, sleep crept up on him, and he let himself drift off with the woman he loved in his arms.

Chapter Twenty-Six

River woke with a start, sat up in bed and looked around in a panic.

It took her a moment to realize where she was. For a split second, she was sure she was dreaming. But then, she felt Cade's hand slide over her waist and pull her in close to his side, and she let out a sigh of relief. No, this was real, she was really here—she was safely back at the lodge with Cade. She had nothing to worry about anymore.

She sank back against the pillow and glanced at the clock on the bedside table. It was nearly two in the morning. She could hardly remember getting back to the cabin at all. She must have fallen asleep in the truck. There was a distant memory of feeling his arms scoop her up as he carried her out into the cold again, but that was it. She'd been so exhausted she could probably have slept for a full day and still been a little out of it. The only thing she remembered about getting home was Hannah being so relieved to see her—crying and hugging her over and over.

River should be sleeping now, but she couldn't. She found herself looking at Cade, staring at him as he slept. She couldn't believe she was really back with him. When Ryker had managed to grab her, she had been so certain there was no way she could get away from him. She had already escaped once, and it seemed impossible she'd be able to do it a second time. She was afraid Cade would be lost to her for good.

And then, she remembered. Ryker was dead. She expected to feel guilty when she thought about what happened, but she didn't. Instead, when she pictured his body lying in the snow, she felt…free. Not like before, when she had first escaped, and she had been certain they were on her trail. She knew he would never come after her again. She was free, and so was the rest of her family.

Her chest tightened when she thought of how much her father would have loved to see this day. She wished he could have, but she knew he would have been proud of her if he were still alive. She had taken out Ryker for good, and there was no way he would be able to come after her again. He was gone. Forever.

She hadn't felt this way in so long, like the weight had been lifted from her shoulders and she could finally just… be. All the fear, all the doubt, all the worry that she was going to bring some kind of chaos to the lodge because of who she was and the life she'd lived before, it was over. She got to look forward to the rest of her life, whatever she wanted that to be.

And right now, all she wanted was to be with Cade. She wanted to lie there in his arms and focus on the joy of knowing she could be totally honest with him. She didn't have to pretend to be anyone she wasn't. She could never have imagined that this was where she would end up, when she'd accepted the ride from him all those weeks ago. She was so glad things had turned out the way they did.

He had come for her. When he had told her he would protect her, he'd meant it. He'd come out into that frigid forest to search for her, even though he knew how dangerous it was and had no idea what he was up against. If it hadn't been for him, God only knew what would have happened with her and Ryker. His sudden appearance was the distraction she'd needed to muster the courage to swing that rock that had saved her life. If it hadn't been for him, she probably still would have been in Ryker's clutches right now.

He'd given her the strength to do what she needed to do to survive, and she was more grateful than she would ever be able to put into words. She supposed she would just have to show him.

She reached out to touch his cheek as he slept, and he stirred, his eyes opening as he looked at her.

"You okay?" he asked, pulling her in closer. Even though the snow was still falling outside, the warmth under these covers, pressed up close to him, was everything she needed.

She nodded. "Yeah, I'm fine," she replied. And she meant it. When she was with him, the enormity of everything that had happened fell away, and she knew she didn't have anything to worry about. She could survive anything this crazy world threw at her, because he was there. He would always be there. No matter how bad things got, she knew he wasn't going anywhere, and she loved him for that.

She loved him.

"I'm just…really happy to be here with you," she continued, running her fingers through his hair. He smiled that gorgeous smile that lit up his whole face, and she felt her stomach twist into a knot. He was so handsome. She had been so fearful before, it had been hard to let go and just focus on how happy he made her. It felt good to be able to focus on him—on *them*.

"Me too," he murmured, and he moved to kiss her on the cheek—just the softest kiss, as though he was still being careful with her. But she didn't want him to be careful with her, not now. She wanted him to treat her like she was his, because she was—she belonged to him, utterly and completely. She wanted to show him that.

She turned her head to kiss him properly, and he didn't need to be told twice. He pulled her closer to him, their bodies pressed together, and he wrapped his arms around her tight. She smiled into the embrace, the covers still tucked around them as he held her. It was like they were in a little bubble, cut off from the rest of the world—as though this was the only thing that mattered right now. And it was. She knew there was a lot of stuff for them to work through—emotions, where they were headed moving forward, plans for the future—a whole lot more for them to talk about and deal with. But in that moment, all she could think about was him.

And how much she wanted this moment to last forever.

Chapter Twenty-Seven

"Morning," Lawson greeted as Cade stepped through the door to his office. Cade had no idea how Lawson was even standing upright at that moment. He had been on his feet for days on end now, catching the last of the Shepards who were still on the run out in the woods. Finally, all of the members of that twisted gang had officially been accounted for.

"Morning," Cade replied, handing Lawson a coffee. He figured he would need it. Lawson took a long, grateful sip, and then slumped into the chair on the other side of the desk.

"How's it going?" Cade asked, carefully. There was so much he wanted to ask about, but he didn't even know where to start. He had spent the last several days taking care of River and shutting out the world, at Lawson's suggestion, though he doubted he would have been able to spend much more than an hour or so away from her side. The thought of how close he'd come to losing her made his stomach turn. He wished they could stay in their little bubble in their cabin forever.

"Well, the Shepards are officially done for," Lawson replied. "With Ryker dead, the rest of them don't have any reason to keep going, and they've turned themselves in.

Most of the lower-level ones in the ranks are turning on each other to try and keep out of jail. I have no idea what the courts are going to decide for them, but that's not our problem."

"What about River?" Cade asked. She was always the first thing on his mind these days, and he would have done anything to make sure that she was safe and happy.

Lawson nodded. "I don't think she's going to have to deal with them any longer," he replied. "The worst it will probably come to is testifying against some of the higher-ranking members in court. I've also requested she be kept out of it all, if possible, since there will be plenty of other ex-Shepards to call on. However, since she did witness her father's murder and kill their leader, she might not have a choice. But again, with the others, she won't be testifying alone."

"Good." Cade sighed. He didn't want her to have to go up against those people again, not if he could keep her from it. She had only just gotten out of it all and he hoped it would be a long time before she was called to testify, if she was at all.

"But we're going to have to figure out what we're going to do with her now," Lawson remarked.

Cade stiffened and furrowed his brow. "What do you mean?"

"I mean, she's going to be sticking around here for a while, isn't she?" he asked.

"I don't know about that."

"I've seen the way she looks at you, Cade." Lawson chuckled. "I don't think she has any intentions of being anywhere else if she can help it."

Cade grinned. He loved being with her, and the thought of being able to spend time with her without having to worry about her past or what she was hiding from him sounded seriously good.

"Exactly," Lawson replied, seeing the look on Cade's face. "And if she's going to continue to stay here, she's going to need real work. She'll need to provide identification and do paperwork like all the other employees. No more under-the-table stuff."

Cade nodded. "Got it. What did you have in mind?"

"I've been talking to Sarah, and she seems to think that with some training, River could help with counseling some of the residents here." he suggested. "But first, she's going to have a whole lot to work through herself."

"I know." Cade sighed.

Sometimes when he looked at her, he wondered how she could be carrying the monstrous weight of everything she had been through inside her. How someone who seemed so fragile could endure what she had without breaking. But she had. He was confident that with the help of the resources at the lodge, she would be able to heal from the trauma of her past and use it to help others. And she would be great at it.

"Let her know that we're interested in hiring her," Lawson told him.

"I will, but I don't want her to feel pressured. Whether she decides to stay or not is up to her." Cade stated.

"I get it," he agreed. "She needs to make her own calls from here on out. Guess she's had enough of other people doing that for her."

"Exactly," Cade replied.

"And what about you, Cade?" Lawson asked, leaning forward with interest.

"What about me?"

"Are you going to stay here?"

Cade parted his lips in surprise. "What do you mean?"

"I mean, you've got a full-time place on the team if you want it," he continued. "But I'm not going to try to make you stay. If you've got other things you want to be doing, we'll see you off—"

"You want me to stay and work for the team?" Cade asked in surprise.

"You helped us take down one of the most dangerous groups in the country," Lawson pointed out. "We're not letting you go anywhere if we can help it. You're a huge asset to us. I'm sure your brother would be thrilled to have you on board, as well."

Cade grinned. There was no way he was going anywhere. Being at the lodge had given him purpose he hadn't had in so long. Not just being with River, but seeing his brother and working with the guys too. He might not be up to the same action he had seen before, but he didn't want to miss out on the chance to find his place here. It was different than his past life and job, but no less rewarding.

"I would love to stay," he replied. "I know my brother's going to try and keep me out of anything too tough, but surveillance, recon, anything like that, you know I can handle it."

"I know you can," Lawson confirmed. "And we'd be glad to have you."

"Consider me a permanent resident," Cade told him with a laugh. "You're not getting rid of me now."

Lawson chuckled in return, rising to his feet, and extended his hand to Cade.

"Welcome aboard, Cade. For real this time."

Cade took his hand. "Thanks, Lawson. Happy to be here."

AFTER THE MEETING with Lawson, Cade stopped by the cafeteria to pick up some coffee and a pastry for River before heading back to the cabin. Though she had physically recuperated from the ordeal after several days of rest, she was still struggling with her appetite, and he had to keep an eye on her to make sure she ate properly. He didn't mind, though. Taking care of her gave him a sense of purpose like nothing else did, as though this was what he had been made for.

When he got back to the cabin, he found her sitting on the couch, several pages laid out around her, with tears streaming down her face.

His eyes widened and his stomach clenched at the sight of her upset. He quickly headed over to the couch and sat down next to her. "Hey," he murmured gently. "Is everything okay?"

She blinked, as though she had almost forgotten where she was, but then she nodded.

"Yes. It's fine," she replied, wiping the tears away from her eyes. "Better than fine, actually. I got an email from my sister. Xavier called in a favor with someone he knows and got me her email address. I think I've already read it a dozen times."

"I just can't believe how well she's doing," River smiled. "She's married now and has a baby. I have a niece, Cade. I can't wrap my head around that. And my mom's there with them too. So they're all together."

"That's amazing news," Cade told her, grabbing a box of tissues and handing her one. He sat back down beside her, draped an arm along the back of the couch and brushed his fingers through her hair.

"It is," she replied. "I can't wait to go and see them now that I don't have to worry about anyone following me or tracking me down. I can actually visit and just spend some time with them. We've got so much to catch up on—it's been nearly ten years!"

She leaned back against his hand, gathering the pages of the letter together again. There was a look on her face he couldn't quite read, a mixture of sadness and hope. She took a deep breath before she said anything else.

"What is it?" he asked.

"I'm just…it's so strange," she confessed. "I've spent the last few years thinking about my family every single day. Thinking that when I got to them, everything was going to be okay. Everything was going to be different. I wasn't going to have to run and hide anymore or look over my shoulder. I could leave everything else behind. But now…" She trailed off, shaking her head.

He rubbed her back softly and waited for her to continue.

She smiled gratefully at him. "Now that Ryker's gone, and the Shepards are disbanded, I don't have to get to them to be safe anymore," she explained. "I want to see my family, of course, but I don't feel as though New York is my endgame. I can have any kind of life I want for myself, and I don't have to try and get to this certain place to make it happen."

She smiled, a smile so huge it seemed to light up her entire face. Cade couldn't help but return it. Seeing the weight lift from her shoulders like this was a gift he didn't even know he had needed until now.

"Whatever you want, I'm here for you," he told her, and he meant it.

He would do anything to help her achieve her dreams. She deserved it, even if it meant she couldn't stay here. She deserved to chase down everything she had always wanted, without the fear of some monster on her tail ready to take it all away.

"I… I think I want to stay here," she confessed, biting her lip as she looked over at him. "Do you think I could do that? I could keep mending up all the clothes to pay my way, I wouldn't—"

A wide grin spread over his face. "Actually, I was just talking to Lawson, and he said that Sarah wants you to work with her. You'd need some training, but she can help with that, and then you can help other people who've been through hardships too. I know you would be amazing at it."

Her eyebrows shot up, and her eyes widened. "Really?" she gasped. "Not under-the-table work, you mean?"

"No, real work," he assured her. "If that's something you want to do, of course."

"I would love to," she exclaimed. "Oh my gosh, I would love to! I really want to help people, Cade. I know there are so many people out there who've been through worse than I have, and I want to help them. I know what it feels like to be afraid…and now I know how it feels to finally be free of it too." She clasped her hands to her chest in excitement.

"And it could help you work through your own stuff,"

he pointed out. "I'm sure there's still plenty you need to figure out."

"I'm sure there is," she admitted. "I just try not to think about it, if I can help it. But I don't want to run from it anymore. I want to face it, and I want to put it behind me for good. And I… I want to make a life for myself. I want to get my GED, I want a real job, and I want to stay here. With you, Cade."

She gazed at him, biting her lip and smiling. Her eyes shone with happy tears.

"I love you, Cade," she breathed to him.

He didn't even have to think before he said it back. "I love you too, River," he replied, and he leaned across to kiss her.

As he pulled her into his arms, he realized that his mind wasn't reeling like he expected it to be the first time he said those words to someone. Loving her was easy. He loved her, she loved him, and she wanted to stay here, with him. It couldn't have made more sense. Or be more perfect.

When he pulled back, she gazed into his eyes for a moment, staring at him like she was trying to figure out if all of this was real. He planted another kiss on her lips, and she smiled, snuggling into him.

"Let's make this place our home, Cade," she whispered to him. "Me and you. Just the two of us."

"Just the two of us," he replied with a chuckle. "Well, and everyone else at the lodge."

She laughed. "I meant in this cabin."

He grinned. "In that case, yeah, just the two of us," he agreed, and he lowered his mouth to hers to kiss her again. He couldn't get enough of her lips on his, the way it made him feel. The way she made him feel as though he was truly whole for the first time. He'd finally found his place and purpose after being sidelined with his injury. He finally felt like he belonged and he was truly happy.

But he would have gone through it all again, and more, if it meant ending up here with her. Where he belonged.

Once and for all.

Epilogue

It was a bright summer's afternoon, the leaves rustling quietly as she followed the familiar path down to the cabin she shared with Cade. Hard to believe it had already been eight months since she'd arrived here, but the turning of the seasons reminded her how much had changed since she had first come to this place in the fall.

And now she might be looking at a whole new start.

With the letter gripped tight in her hand, River hurried, hoping Cade would be there when she arrived. She didn't want to wait any longer than she already had to open this thing, but she had promised she wouldn't check her application until he was back.

She wasn't sure how much longer she could contain herself. She felt as though she was going to explode as she stepped into the cabin and looked around—no sign of Cade yet.

She sank down on the couch with an impatient sigh and pressed the letter into her legs, looking down at it again. The Chapel Hill logo was on the top right corner, and she was sure this was it, the letter that would either confirm or deny she'd made it in to the university of her dreams.

Heading to town earlier in the day to pick up some supplies, she had stopped in at their post office box and found it waiting for her. She knew Cade was away doing some training with guys from the lodge, so she promised herself that she wouldn't open it until he was there with her to see what the letter said. She was regretting that promise right about now because all she wanted to do was rip the envelope open.

What if she had been rejected? She couldn't help but wonder how she would feel. She had put so much stock into this moment, into getting accepted by the school, that she could hardly believe it was finally here. Today she would find out one way or another what the next phase of her life was going to look like.

Terrifying? Completely. But she had long since learned that she could take a lot more of the scary stuff than she had ever imagined she could.

She had managed to get her GED, and had spent the better part of the spring writing endless essays and filling out applications to every university in the area. She wanted to become a Licensed Professional Counselor, and even though it was going to be a long journey, she had to start somewhere. Chapel Hill had been her first pick from day one, but she had never really let herself believe she would actually get accepted. Staring at this letter that would decide her fate, she found herself wondering how she would feel if, just maybe, she had actually done it.

Finally, she heard Cade arrive. Good. She needed him by her to get through this.

"What's going on?" he asked, as he went to make himself a coffee.

River held up the letter. "It's from Chapel Hill," she explained.

His eyes widened. "Did you get in?"

"I haven't opened it yet," she admitted. "I wanted to wait until you were here."

"Well, what are you waiting for?" he demanded, grinning widely. "Go for it!"

She had been so excited, almost bouncing off the walls, but now she hesitated. She didn't know if she could. Now that she'd had time to think about it, the fear was starting to creep in.

"You open it," she told Cade, handing the letter over to him. He took it from her, and she chewed her lip and watched his face as he slowly opened it.

A smile spread over his face. "You got in!" he exclaimed, and she let out a shriek.

"You're serious?" She snatched the letter from him, skimming through it. Sure enough, he was telling the truth—they had offered her a place to study psychology, starting in the fall. She clapped a hand over her mouth, hardly able to contain herself. It was such an amazing feeling. She wanted to run and tell everyone she'd done it.

"I knew you would," Cade told her, scooping her up into his arms and kissing her firmly on the lips.

She laughed and hugged him back. "I need to call Haven to tell her the good news."

"Absolutely," He replied. "You do that and I'll go rustle up some grub from the cafeteria so we can have a celebratory dinner tonight."

"Sounds like a plan," she said, planting a quick kiss on his mouth. "Thank you."

She talked to Haven for the next half hour via video chat, sharing her good news and just catching up. Even though River had yet to make it to New York because of school, getting her GED, working on college applications, and everything going on around the lodge, she and her sister spoke every day. Sometimes her mom joined in too.

Their first conversations were so emotional it had taken several calls to just get through the basics of what had happened over the years and not cry every other word. But how wonderful it had been to see her mother and sister and to meet her niece! Now they spoke regularly and made plans to visit each other soon. Just knowing that her family was safe and they had a wonderful life meant the world to River.

The next day Cade had planned a hike with their friends from the lodge. They packed a picnic and hit the trail that ran into the woods and up to a viewpoint over the town below. It was a beautiful day as they set out together.

Hannah walked with her and Cade nearly the whole way. "You've done so well, River. You should be so proud of yourself. I'm so glad you'll be staying here and doing classes remotely—double win!"

"Me too," River replied, grinning widely as Cade gave her hand a squeeze. They'd both agreed that doing her university coursework while living at Warrior Peak Sanctuary would be the best of all possible worlds.

"Sad that you won't get in your wild partying years?" Hannah asked playfully.

River laughed and shook her head. "Not when my other option is staying here with Cade. I'll take that over partying any day. He's all I want."

He looked over at her fondly and winked, and then glanced over his shoulder, seeing the guys fall behind.

"Hey, keep up, guys!" he called to them, and he dropped back to match their pace, leaving Hannah and River alone.

"You want to wait for them?" River asked.

"No, let's keep walking," she replied, looking downward.

River lowered her voice. "Is everything okay?"

"I don't even know," she sighed. "I'm not even sure where to start. I feel like I'm going crazy. It's been months, and I don't know what I'm supposed to do with all of it."

"With all of what?"

"With the way I feel about Xavier," she admitted. "It's just…it all feels like such a mess, that's all. With Xavier kissing me and Lawson finding out, then the two of them arguing… Everything seems so strained now between us all." She trailed off, and then shook her head.

"I'm sorry, this day is supposed to be about celebrating you," she added. "Let's not talk about my stuff. It's all so jumbled right now."

"I don't mind talking about your stuff, but I understand," River replied. "Just know you can always come to me if you need someone to talk to."

"Hey, you're already acting like a therapist." Hannah joked. "You're going to be at the top of your class in no time, I can feel it!"

River giggled. She was still trying to wrap her head around the fact she had actually made it into the school of her dreams. It all felt so surreal, when she thought about where she had been this time last year. Out on the road, alone and scared, fighting to get to her family, constantly looking over her shoulder because she was terrified that Ryker would find her.

She never would have imagined she would feel this free and be this happy. She felt ready to take on the world. She didn't have to stay on the run or worry for her life or the lives of anyone she cared about. Discovering who she really was underneath the programming of the Shepards and the fear and pain they had inflicted on her had been a joy.

Cade caught up with them again and slipped his hand into hers. He always held her hand when they were out and she loved it. It was like he wanted to make sure she was always next to him. She didn't want to be anywhere else. She smiled over at him, the warmth of the sunshine bathing her face for a moment as he gazed back at her.

Hannah fell back with the guys for a while, and River looked over her shoulder to see how it was going. Carter was chatting with Hannah, while Lawson and Xavier were off to the side and seemed uncomfortable. River hoped they'd be able to work it all out.

But before she could mention it to Cade, he pointed over to the side. "Look, we're at the viewpoint."

He was right. They had already reached the spot that looked down over the town below. The sun shone through the trees around them, a soft breeze stirring the leaves, and the sky so blue above them it seemed to go on forever.

"It's so beautiful up here," she breathed, leaning her head against his shoulder for a moment. They had come up here a lot since the weather had started to warm up. It had become one of her favorite spots, and it was a perfect place to celebrate getting accepted into college.

"It is," he murmured, turning toward her. The look on his face shifted to something more serious.

He took a deep breath. "River, there's something I wanted to ask you," he said, sliding his hand into his pocket.

"What? Is everything okay?"

"More than okay," he assured her, smiling. "I… These last few months, they've been some of the happiest of my life. Being with you, it's given me a purpose like nothing else. And I want to spend the rest of my life fulfilling that purpose—being here for you, supporting you and loving you while you achieve everything you were meant to achieve."

Her lips parted in surprise. She wasn't sure where this had come from, but when he pulled a small blue box from his pocket, it clicked. She felt a wave of dizziness rush over her and she pressed hand against her stomach to stop the butterflies. He dropped to one knee right there on the grass before her and opened up the box. The diamond sparkled in the sunshine.

He looked up at her, his eyes shining with love. "River, will you marry me?"

"Oh my gosh! Of course I will!" she shrieked, and she pulled him to his feet and leaped into his arms.

He laughed, pulling back just long enough to slip the ring over her finger, and then squeezed her against him once more.

"I love you, River," he told her. "And I'm going to spend the rest of my life making sure you know how much I mean that."

"I love you too," she breathed back, and she kissed him again.

As their friends congratulated them and she showed Hannah her ring, she felt content and so excited for a future she never could have dreamed for herself. A life she couldn't wait to experience with the man she adored right by her side.

* * * * *

Look for more books in USA TODAY
bestselling author Janie Crouch's miniseries,
Warrior Peak Sanctuary, coming soon,
only from Harlequin Intrigue!